Cleansing Blade Saga 3

Merciless Destinies

Randolph Ashby

Acknowledgments:

This book is dedicated to;

My son, always know that through your faith and people who love you, you can accomplish anything and overcome any obstacle.

Special thanks to;

Rhonda and Rachel, thank you for the work you have put in.

Chapter 1: Prologue

All my life, *I have fought for the rights of others. To serve and protect. Expecting nothing in return but more service. But betrayal is all I have received. First, my own government hunted me down and now, I fear that my own creation has realized that I may be the next one on their list of targets. Zamora fell, then Camelot at their hands. Reaper, why is it so hard for you to see things? Romeo, my pity upon you, I feel the hatred you have for me. Violet, I saw more potential in you than the rest. As for the non-Cleansing Blade recruits, I have lost all trust.*

Betrayal is all I have seen. Even those I considered my children have now forsaken all their values and loyalties. They proved their rights of passage at that school. I made sure they would rise to the challenge and become what I meant would save the world. I did not seek vengeance, nor did I seek fortune. I saw only the right to use the power I had for the better of mankind. Perhaps, I have failed them.

Boss, I understand your decision to remain at their side. We have seen much. I know it was your better judgement to stay with them. Their naivety is humoring and you still see things their way. I must have been the only one to be enlightened. My enemies were what I once called my friends, my comrades, my children. Cleansing Blade served their purpose in stopping my old enemies, but now with the feeling of accomplishment, they seek to root out the rest of the old Lazer Blade. As if drunk with power, they now seek to conquer. They are coming for me.

I wish the Academy would have taught them something more than to hold a grudge. I saved them from a lowlife future. I gave them the skills they needed to protect the innocent. But all in vain, as the deaths of my old comrades, and now mine, have come to pass. I know they blame me for the tragedies that befell them at the campus grounds. For that, it was part of their initiation. Accept and move on. It is clear to me that only one has seen that; Violet, dear sweet child, thank you.

I bestowed my best upon you all, and have once again expected nothing in return. The horror I've seen in mankind, is personified in Romeo. I hope that at the very least, you do not lose your way. That Cleansing Blade, or whatever you may call yourselves now, can stick to the path that I set out for you.
Remember my words; an uncertain hero is far more dangerous than even the relentless villain.

Philip Johnson

Reaper lay wide awake staring at the ceiling of his quarters. He heard the soothing sound of the Nest vents circulating air inside the facility. It was going to be another night without sleep. Light seeping in from the hallway crept through the door and gently lit a poster of an aurora borealis pinned onto the ceiling. The image of hovering lights lay just over a mountain pass. He took a deep breath and fell back into his thoughts. Aurora, his fellow comrade, had given her life protecting others. The thought of it made him sick. According to Provost's suicide letter, he made it sound like it was all for nothing and that all of the team's previous endeavors had somehow pitted them against him. The words of his former leader rattled Reaper's mind.

For nearly a year, the Shadows of the Sun fulfilled their duties, trained a new recruit, and continued to follow leads to Provost's whereabouts. Old hideouts that Boss informed the team about were the only clues they had to go on. No sign of Provost in any of them. Reaper trusted Boss and his intel. He had no reason to think otherwise, even under the circumstances. Boss had stuck by the team, even giving them information on Provost's darkest secrets. Being the only surviving and remaining Lazer Blade member was sure to put massive pressure on Boss. Reaper understood it as much as he could. Provost was his family too, though the bond was different. The Academy brought out the worst in Provost but for the best in the Cleansing Blade. Through that, Reaper learned that Provost's approach was a type of tough love. It was a way to break them and rebuild them into something stronger.

Could Provost have run in fear? Or was it another test? Another form of tough love. Reaper heard the hollow and empty walls of the Nest suddenly fill with a set of footsteps. He snapped out of his thoughts to find out who was up in the middle of the night. Perhaps he was not the only one fighting for sleep. He got out of his bed and walked over to the door. The cool air brushed by his naked torso. Wearing only sweatpants, he opened the doors to the brightly lit hallway. The clapping of feet against the cold floor echoed down the hall, they were careful, sharp and slow. Reaper glanced to see fiery red hair brush down the hallway. The tall woman turned to enter the lounge. Reaper smiled in admiration, amazed she could navigate as well as any "normal" person.

Reaper proceeded towards the lounge, quick and steady. He opened the door slowly to see what she was up to. The tall fiery redhead stood above a bowl of almonds. Reaper was proud of his newest recruitment choice. The florescent light made her light skin glow. And she was exceptionally coordinated for being blind. Her eyes were filled with a strangely beautiful marble color that filled the entire eyeball. Her smooth complexion was clearly visible since she was wearing nothing but a sports top and shorts. Fit and sharp, she was a great addition to the team.

"How long are you going to stare at me?" She spoke, startling Reaper out of his trance.

"Uh, um," Reaper knew he was busted, "Oracle....."

"You're making me uncomfortable." Oracle replied.

"Sorry." Reaper proceeded inside the lounge. "I didn't mean to make you nervous." He approached her slowly. "Restless?"

Oracle finished chewing, "Hunger pains. I get them sometimes late at night."

Reaper watched her eat, "Can't say I get those kinds of pains."

"Restless again? I can see it in your face." She gazed through him, as if noticing his dark rings under his eyes.

Reaper was constantly amazed by her. Though blind, she claimed to be able to see. An infection in her eyes as a child rendered them useless. The lush marble color was alluring. She even claimed to be psychic. Reading thoughts and foretelling the near future. Inducted as a member of the Shadows of the Sun just two months before, she proved to be everything he had hoped for. Stunning everybody on the team, she made it look easier to dodge a bullet than even the quick reflexes of Romeo. With the help of the Adrenaline Solution, her remaining senses were heightened to a level Reaper had never seen before. After just two months, she had nearly finished her training and conditioning. Impressive was an understatement. With her, Reaper felt confident again.

"Thinking of Provost? Or Aurora?" Oracle asked as she smiled.

Reaper showed his amazement by laughing nervously, "Both."

She seemed to study him, "I can hear your mind. No wonder you can't find sleep."

Reaper moved to sit at the table next to her, fearing to open up too much, he allowed himself to spill some of his thoughts. "I guess I'm letting this investigation get to me. It's personal."

Oracle moved to the table to join him, she sat across moving into her chair with slow precision. "I think you are scared of something."

"Like what?" Reaper asked, confused.

"Fear is something we must all come to face." She finished her bowl of almonds, "You fear that Provost may have moved on."

"What do you mean?"

Oracle looked through him, "He moved on to something besides this, Cleansing Blade."

"That's not it," Reaper snapped, "If I'm afraid, it's because he might be doing something crazy or he actually carried out his objective by killing himself for no reason."

"And you fear not having had closure." she concluded.

Reaper said nothing, perhaps she was right.

"Reaper, you must think." Oracle said softly.

"About what?" Reaper felt exposed.

"The beginning may lead to the answers."

Reaper looked puzzled, "Beginning?"

Oracle swayed her head as if looking around the room, her movements were like a tree in the wind. It was only the verification Reaper needed to know he named her accordingly. She was getting to the point of her statement, hopefully. He knew she tended to speak in obscure statements.

"Oracle, please," Reaper was losing his patience.

She gazed at him. "Reaper, the beginning is where the answer may lie."

"Oracle, I'm still not used to your riddles." Reaper said.

"You've searched in his shadow." She continued, "Now you must search in yours."

Reaper held his tongue to process her words. He knew she meant well. But the process was dragging. "The beginning of our shadow?" he thought out loud.

"Exactly." Oracle said with a smile. "You see now?"

Reaper searched for the answer. His shadow, Provost's hideouts? Reaper thought more, then finally, "The Academy!?"

Oracle stood up and proceeded to the sink where she grabbed a glass of water. "I'm headed back to bed." She turned to look at Reaper who seemed to regain his confidence. "I hope you can sleep well."

Reaper turned to her, "Not so fast." He moved to the door, "We have a mission to commence."

Shadows of the Sun Roster....Updating

Accessing Roster...

Member Name: Reaper

Age: 26

Height: 5 ft 10in

Weight: 165lbs

Eyes/Hair: Reddish Brown/Black

Emphasis: Leadership, Handguns, Infiltration, GSK Proficient.

Bio: Reaper carries the burden of his team solely on his shoulders. Primarily the death of his fellow teammate, Aurora. Though he trusts his team to accomplish whatever task at hand, he still feels the need to take it upon himself to be responsible for their actions. While he still has Cleansing Blade disbanded and formed into the Shadows of the Sun, the team stands by him 110%. With the suicide letter of Provost memorized, he is restless to find out what happened to his former leader.

Member Name: Violet

Age: 25

Height: 5 ft 7 in

Weight: 125lbs

Eyes/Hair: Green/Blond

Emphasis: Automatic pistols, Moral Support, GSK Proficient.

Bio: Violet has faith, plain and simple. Faith in God, her team, and humanity. Her values for human life set the boundaries for the team to not be just another group of mercenaries. She supports the team in ways of lifting moral when times get rough. It pleases her to know that Reaper and the others do their best to honor her wishes not to kill needlessly. She believes in mercy for the enemy. Emotions run high inside her as she finds herself slowly getting closer to Amraam. Given their experiences together, she finds comfort in him.

Member Name: Romeo

Age: 27

Height: 5 ft 9 in

Weight: 170lbs

Eyes/Hair: Brown/Dark Brown.

Emphasis: Knives, Hand to hand, infiltration, GSK Proficient.

Bio: Romeo holds on to the demons of his past. From his time at the Academy. His dagger is a constant reminder of that place. And his promise to 'Live' inscribed on the blade. The word his love told him in her dying breath. Since then, his resentment for Provost has only worsened as he blames him for the negligent events at the Academy. Uneasy with Reaper's authority as well, Romeo keeps his distance towards feeling any sort of emotion on or off the battlefield.

Member Name: Crosshair

Age: 25

Height: 6 ft 4 in

Weight: 230lbs

Eyes/Hair: Green/Light Brown

Emphasis: Sniper, long range weapons, GSK trained.

Bio: If anyone has the pressure of watching over the team, it's Crosshair. At a distance, he supports the team through his scope and a keen eye in reconnaissance. With his new customized goggles strapped to his head, he surveys everything in front of him. Spending his time in solo operating side missions lately, Crosshair has kept many questionable locations under close eye as instructed by Reaper. Though lately he has thoughts of his childhood home.

Member Name: Aurora

Status: Deceased

Bio: Aurora lives on in the mind of Reaper. He claims to have seen her in the form of an Aurora Borealis. Though no one can confirm this. Reaper holds her close to his heart. To him, she is alive in spirit.

Member Name: Circuitcrusher

Age: 26

Height: 6 ft 1 in.

Weight: 240lbs.

Eyes/Hair: Blue/Light Brown

Emphasis: Electronics, Gadgets, Communications. GSK trained.

Bio: Circuitcrusher, a man summed up in one word simply cannot be done. Known as Circue (Sir-q) in the field, he is responsible for working on new technology and gadgets for the team. His admiration for pilots is shown by wearing his pilot headphones around his neck. Proud of his inventions, he is very savvy when it comes to helping the team work in the cyber battlefield of data. Working alongside Motherboard at times keeps him pushing to improve. Causing an uneasy truce among them in the fight of cyber warfare.

Member Name: Monster

Age: 27

Height: 6 ft 6 in

Weight: 280lbs

Eyes/Hair: Dark Brown/Black

Emphasis: Heavy Weapons, Support Operations, GSK Proficient.

Bio: When muscle is needed to accomplish a mission, Monster is the man. A staggering size and surprising grace, he is an asset in bringing in the big guns and providing the necessary support the team needs when things get crazy. Keeping his long thick hair tied back in a handkerchief and a firm grip on a machinegun, only the foolish stand in his way willingly. He normally travels with Circuitcrusher to keep him safe and give the tech guy more things to worry about.

Member Name: Gothica

Age: 33

Height: 5 ft 9in

Weight: 120lbs

Eyes/Hair: Blue/Brown

Emphasis: Infiltration, Stealth, GSK Proficient

Bio: Gothica contains much more field experience than the rest. As her former profession was an efficient CIA agent, she specializes in stealth tactics and sneaking without leaving a trace. Her crossbow pistol is either on her side or in her hand. Through her mentorship and advice, Reaper keeps her close when preparing for missions. Though not an original member of the Cleansing Blade, her loyalty remains with them.

Member Name: Amraam

Age: 32

Height: 6 ft. 0 in.

Weight: 180lbs

Eyes/Hair: Brown/Black

Emphasis: Close quarters combat, weapons expert, Grab Smash Kill (GSK) proficient.

Bio: Amraam is a soldier by heart. He wears his bandana wrap on his head from his Special Forces days. And he always enters battle with his trusty P90 submachine gun in hand. From his experiences with the Shadows of the Sun, Amraam's determination has been boosted as well as his intent to protect his team at any cost. Though relationships and feelings are shunned in the unit, Amraam has grown quite fond of fellow teammate, Violet. Years of being with and around her have made the hard work in the field worthwhile.

Member Name: Radical

Age: 30

Height: 5 ft 11 in

Weight: 170lbs

Eyes/Hair: Hazel/Brown

Emphasis: Explosives, Demolition, GSK Trained.

Bio: If anyone can blow a situation out of proportion, it's Radical. Enthralled by explosives and the will to make enemies run and scream, he always wears a detonation cord around his wrists and keeps his lucky dynamite fuse in his pocket. Though he may undermine Reaper at times, he knows he trusts his ability to accomplish the mission and cripple the enemy.

Member Name: Motherboard

Age: 23

Height: 5 ft 3 in

Weight: 110lbs

Eyes/Hair: Hazel/Dark Brown

Emphasis: Computer and cyber warfare, hacking, GSK trained.

Bio: Motherboard's only weapon is her custom made mission data pad. With it, anyone posing a threat to the digital world of cyberspace can be stopped by her fast fingers and knowledge of software and its many constricting qualities. When something must be entered or unlocked via electronics, she will get it done in the blink of an eye. Though her counterpart, Circue, will disagree. She has become well-adjusted to the team's habits and fearlessly steps into the field whenever she is needed.

Member Name: Oracle

Age: 31

Height: 5 ft 10 in

Weight: 130lbs

Eyes/Hair: Marble/Red

Emphasis: Infiltration, telepathic, psychic, GSK trained

Bio: Oracle is a remarkable human being. Blinded as a child by an unknown infection, her eyes are completely engulfed by a marble shell. She claims to have the ability to read minds and has even claimed to see into the near future. Reaper hand-picked her from a military research facility. She took well to the ways of the Shadows of the Sun at an exceptionally fast rate. Her tactics and speaking in riddles earns her the name, Oracle.

Section 1:

The Academy

Chapter 2

The briefing room was cool and darker than usual since all computer screens were shut off. Not even the large center console hologram was on. Reaper was dressed in updated attire. The refined sneaking suit was leaner, slicker. Not to mention the flexible touch screen pad now strapped to his wrist, thanks to Circuitcrusher. The sneaking suit had some scuff marks from previous missions. His vest was fastened tightly and he made sure his hi-cap pistol was strapped to his leg. His reddish brown eyes scanned the room and noticed Oracle standing in the back against the table. She remained in her sleepwear of a sports top and shorts which made Reaper struggle to concentrate on the mission briefing. He caught himself staring at her again, but knew he would be caught. Getting to know her more and more caused an attraction to her as time went by. It was going to be difficult to hide these emotions from her. After all, she was psychic. Instead, Reaper shifted his thoughts to the mission. It always worked. He needed Oracle to help in convincing the rest of the selected team members on his new lead. Oracle rubbed her arms as Reaper kept observing her. Then the door swung open with Romeo stumbling towards the center console.

"I like my coffee black as night and strong as iron," Romeo grumbled, "Especially since I got dragged out of the sack before one in the morning." Reaper watched him take a sip and gritted from the heat of the liquid. "So this better be good." Romeo snickered.

Reaper tried to come up with something reassuring, "It could be, but you're probably not going to like it."

Romeo looked over at Oracle who was still rubbing her arms, "You cold?"

Oracle took a second to respond, "This floor is cool."

Romeo laughed as he noticed she was not wearing shoes then looked back up at her chest, "Yeah I can tell, it must be cool in here."

"I'll be fine." Oracle smiled.

Reaper knew Romeo had his qualms with her. Maybe it was jealously of her skills. Or maybe it was just Romeo being Romeo, since he did not like anybody.

Romeo turned his torso to stretch, but accidently spilled some of his hot coffee, "Awe, dammit."

"Nice going, need your Sippy cup?"

Reaper smiled at Gothica's comment as she made her way into the room. Her long loose hair was tied back as usual. She was dressed in her sneaking suit and her weapon of choice strapped to her thy.

Romeo came back, "Great, just what I wanted to see this morning. Your pale face."

Gothica was ever quick with her sarcastic comments to combat the always snide Romeo, "I'll still never feel as bad as you look in the mornings."

Reaper interrupted, "Just fall in, please." He shook his head. He was expecting two more. Then the door opened and they entered, Violet and Crosshair.

"Good morning everyone," Violet sounded cheerful.

"Still need your sugar fix this morning to realize it's not?" Romeo teased about her coffee blend she preferred.

Violet held onto her hair as it dangled from her right shoulder. Although it was early, she always seemed to find time to make sure her hair was done in a tight braid. "I plan on fixing me a cup right now."

Gothica could not resist, "Guess his cup of turpentine hasn't kicked in yet."

"Hey," Romeo defended, "This stuff will put hair on your face. Not that you need anymore." He giggled.

Gothica made a face at him.

Crosshair butted in, "Where is everyone else?"

Reaper placed his hands on the center console, "I only buzzed your rooms. This is all we need." He turned to signal Oracle who seemed to look around the room. "Oracle, I need your assistance."

"I know," She responded.

Gothica spoke up, "So what has us lucky few here, is this regarding Provost or something?"

Reaper took a deep breath. "Yes. I have some intel."

Romeo laughed, "You mean, vision girl pointed something out?"

Violet remained silent as she observed the mysterious woman.

Reaper continued, "Something like that. Look, I don't know how to say this, but we may have been looking in the wrong places."

"Reaper seems to have a strong intuition." Oracle supported him. "I just lead him to realize it."

"If that's the case," Romeo was sarcastic as he took another sip.

Violet noticed Reaper was disturbed, "Is everything okay?"

Reaper cleared his throat, "I want us to check out a lead. We need to verify any and all locations that Provost may have been to. That means our next stop, is at the Academy."

The room was still.

Gothica interrupted, "Sounds like a decent place to get back into the hunt for him."

"It could be. Just not sure if it'll be a fun reunion going back home." Reaper looked at her.

She responded, "Sometimes, going back home can be a wonderful thing."

"Your home was not the Academy." Reaper told her, sounding depressed.

Oracle looked over at him, "I sense something."

Reaper's heart sped up when he heard her words.

She continued, "Something dark is there." She looked at the others. "Almost like a ghost."

Crosshair replied, glancing at the silent Romeo, "There'd be a few there. That's for sure."

"I cannot see anymore. I'm sorry." Oracle spoke softly as she looked at Reaper.

"You've done well. Thank you, Oracle." Reaper felt assured. "Go back to your room. I'll let you know what happens when we return."

"Good luck to you." Oracle proceeded slowly out the door. Able to navigate with ease.

Romeo remained silent as he took another sip, slowly this time.

Violet sounded nervous, "Shouldn't we have more hands on this? What about Amraam, or anyone else?"

"Didn't feel like briefing more on the location," Reaper tried to comfort them, "Don't worry, it's just a quick in and out. We'll be back before dawn."

"Why didn't we look at this place before?" Gothica asked.

"Cause it's a horrible place." Romeo mumbled and left the room.

Reaper watched him, then looked at the rest, "Gothica, you're the only one going that has no emotional ties to this. I'm counting on you to stay that way. As for the rest of us, we need this. Perhaps, it's closure." He said with uncertainty.

"Why not Circue or Monster?" Gothica observed.

"No need for extra resources. And Circue has work to do here anyway." Reaper noticed Violet stroking her hair excessively. It was her way of showing she was nervous. "Violet, can you handle this?"

She groped her braid, "Yes, let's get going."

Gothica was persistent with questions, "And Boss?"

"He doesn't need to know we're there unless we find something." Reaper assured. "I want this to be low profile. It's just a reconnaissance mission."

Gothica smiled at him, "Cheer up. At least you're following your intuition after all."

Reaper grinned, "Yeah. But don't worry. I'll keep out of everybody's way once we're there."

Crosshair walked towards the door, "What a reunion if he's there huh?"

Reaper looked up at him, "If he's still alive."

With that, the team exited the room and headed for the Ark. The engineering feat was waiting to transport the few members to the destination that Reaper knew would rock the core members of Cleansing Blade. It was their birthplace. It was their new beginning.

Chapter 3

The humming of the Ark engines soothed Romeo in and out of sleep. The red lights in the cabin gave him more of a headache. As to why Reaper wanted him to tag along on this mission was hard to comprehend at the moment. He remembered what had happened there. Julia's death, and Provost's disregard for the loss had brought his blood to a boil. Romeo was struggling with the thought of going back. He gave Reaper a dirty look. His stomach churned at the thought of stepping foot one more time on the Academy grounds. The stress was building up as he adjusted his head to rest it against his locker. Exhaustion was closing in. The flight would give him a little time to catch up on sleep.

The humming continued, but then the sound slowly faded into birds chirping and air brushing past Romeo's ear. His hand felt another that had brought him joy. The Academy grounds were lit up by the lunchtime sun. Romeo knew he was back; a hint of joy entered his heart as he turned to notice her, Julia, the love of his life. She seemed to glow in the sunlight. It put him uneasy seeing her in her favorite red shirt. Casual school attire was allowed at the Academy. No uniforms necessary. Her rosy cheeks complemented her brown hair and eyes. Her short stature made her absolutely adorable. He would have died for her.

He was entranced while she spoke, "So today is Friday. We have permission to see a movie or leave the campus grounds tonight for a few hours." Her voice had brought him peace. Provost had his weekly announcements to the students. For now, they were about promoting a positive future. But Romeo had a dark feeling hovering over him. It was still a dream, but he seemed to be reliving the moments. It made him weak and vulnerable.

The two continued down the side walk. The warm wind brushed past his ear. Romeo noticed a young blond girl sitting on a bench reading a book. She was alone and moving her flailing blond hair from her face. She looked up at them and smiled, acknowledging Julia's friendly wave. Romeo nodded and smiled back, but Julia pulled him over to say hello.

"Hey there," Julia gave her a hug. "What are you up to?"

"Oh, just enjoying a beautiful day." The girl's soft voice spoke up as she placed her book upon her lap. "And taking a break from studying." Romeo knew that this girl, Violet, would one day work alongside him. "And how are you doing, sir?" She asked politely.

"Doing well, actually." Romeo's voice was cheerful and relaxed. "Just another day here in paradise."

Violet smiled and looked upwards, "Don't know about that."

"It's close enough. We're getting a second chance here and all." Romeo looked over at the book in her hands. "Reading anything good?"

Violet lifted her book up, "Oh just, my inspiration for the day. You know, gotta stay inspired." She held up her book of inspirational literature.

Romeo smiled and shook his head, "Whatever helps you make it through the day."

"At least you're trying," Julia commented, "Sometimes we need inspiration to make it through questionable times." She squeezed Romeo's hand.

"Yeah I know," he laughed, "But for now, school smarts are what are gonna get us out of here."

Julia shrugged her shoulders, "You're hopeless." She said playfully.

Violet laughed and looked up at him, "I'm sure the project assignment for next week will be easy. Plus this program will give us something to look forward to in a few months."

"Yeah, we're excited." Julia jumped. "We have our plans in order after we graduate. Hopefully travel and building our own house."

Romeo laughed and pulled her in close, "Whoa, calm down. One step at a time."

Violet giggled, "Sounds like you guys have it all figured out."

"What about you?" Julia insisted, "What do you want to do?"

Violet swiped her hair to the side, "I'd like to travel, too. Maybe do some work in other countries. Peace corps. Who knows."

"That sounds like it could be adventurous. By the way, I love your hair." Julia said as she watched Violet struggle with it in the breeze.

Violet looked surprised, "Thank you."

"Alright you two." Romeo interrupted and pulled Julia closer to him, "Let's leave her alone."

"Hey maybe we can hang out later?" Julia asked.

"Um," Violet hesitated, "Sure."

Julia smiled at her, "You'll have to let me braid your hair."

Violet laughed as she moved it from her face. "Thank you. Yeah I need to do something with it. So yeah, you can braid it."

"Great, we'll be in the student center tonight if you want to meet us there." Julia was excited.

Romeo pulled her towards the walkway, "I guess we'll see you later." Violet waved as the two began walking towards the student quarters. Romeo looked at Julia and shook his head. "Social butterfly."

Julia giggled, "Hey, I'm just trying to make some friends while we're here. She looks like an interesting person. Can't wait, I wish I had long hair..."

Romeo smiled but the vision soon faded. The sky around him turned to red and Julia began to fade as her stomach began bleeding. "Julia?" He tried to yell, but could not. "Julia..."

"Are you okay?" a familiar voice asked. Julia's lips moved but it sounded like Violet talking. A loud ping awoke him from his dream. He panted as sweat poured down his face.

"Are you doing okay?" Violet asked him as the Ark made an adjustment from slight turbulence.

Romeo came to and realized he was back inside the marvel transport. The Ark engines were fueled by nuclear energy, giving it an unlimited amount of power. The automated pilot system allowed for more cargo space in the cabin. It was the main transport in getting the team quickly to the mission area. It was only ten more minutes until they hit the grounds of the old Academy. Romeo's heart sped up with anxiety. He looked to acknowledge Violet. "Yeah, I'm fine." He stood up and walked past her, looking for the small infirmary on the Ark. He walked towards the sink and turned the water on to splash some water across his face and grabbed the nearest towel. After padding down his face he looked into the small mirror above the faucet. The lights in the cabin made his face reflect the red. The mirror started to shake as the red lights lit his eyes up.

Romeo once again found himself at the Academy looking into the eyes of Reaper. The slight red tint in his eyes brought a sort of unsteadiness to Romeo. It was the day after the big announcement from the Provost. The Academy was slowly becoming a prison.

"I noticed you have someone. The more we have the better." Reaper said quietly. "This place is going to hell, soon."

"What do you think we should do?" Romeo held Julia tight to his side, the small dorm room was quiet. "It's not like we can sneak out of here that easy."

"I know," Reaper took a second as he placed his hand on his chin, "We need to plan a diversion. It would need to be big enough for us to slip away."

"But the teachers?" Julia cut in, "What about them?"

"We have to assume they're all in on it." Reaper tried to consolidate, "Just stick with some of the students. There's that tall guy and that really smart kid that hang out in the cafeteria. Maybe even that other girl you guys know. The blondie?"

"Yeah, we can talk to her." Romeo said, "I met another guy here, a tall guy who's always looks at hunting magazines."

Reaper nodded, "I know another girl," He stepped back and signaled someone to enter the room. "This is Catherine. We've been getting to know each other and both came to the same conclusion about getting out."

Catherine stood next to Reaper and stuck her hand out to shake. Romeo felt his heart sink as he remembered her. Her lightly freckled face seemed to glow with confidence. Romeo recalled her as, Aurora. Her brains matched her beauty and her presence was comforting. The four of them started to plan. It was only a matter of time before the Provost made the staff become excessively violent towards the students. Romeo could feel the hope building. Could this guy and girl really make a plan that would get them all out? Romeo recalled Aurora's strength and attitude. When she would sometimes keep Reaper in check. He found himself actually missing her.

Chapter 4

Romeo found himself fading deeper into his flashback. It was almost as if an entity had taken hold and made him watch. The day before he met with Reaper and Aurora, he recalled the speech made by the Provost. Goosebumps arose on his skin. It was the speech that changed everything.

Within the campus walls, the students had all filed into the center of the courtyard at attention. The Provost stood at the podium in the front of the courtyard. Dressed and clean cut, his golden hair slicked back and his gray eyes hard as stone. Five other staff members were present and dressed in uniforms assembled on stage with him. Fifteen staff in uniform stood throughout the assembly of 47 students. The Provost approached the microphone and laid his hands upon the podium.

"I have called you all here to give you a sort of, well, redirection as to how things will be handled around here. As you all may have heard, one of your fellow students was struck while in detention. And I will have you know, this will not be the first time that this is going to happen."

All of the students stood still. Romeo's eyes widened. He moved them slightly towards the direction where Julia stood a few rows down. He could not believe what he was hearing. What he once doubted and heard rumors about was now confirmed by the man running the Academy. Romeo gritted his teeth as the speech continued.

"Now, I will tell you how things are going to work. If you arrive to class late, you will face punishment. This punishment may include beatings, or even therapy to help lighten up your attitude. If you backtalk to one of the staff, you will also receive therapy and will be given some good, hard labor to help hold your tongue. And finally, if you are late a second time, you will be taken out into the desert and restrained for a day without food or water. And with this nice hot summer weather out here, it shall prove to be, well, as you young people put it…loads of fun. Thank you, and now you may all go to your classes. Oh, and remember, don't be late."

The Provost finished his speech, and the staff began chasing the students to get them to hustle out of the courtyard. The Provost proceeded to walk down the stairs of the stage and disappeared out of sight.

Romeo was awakened by another jolt from the Ark making a slight correction. He looked around to notice the team was still around the cabin getting their things ready for the drop. Reaper was at the console looking at images of the now vacant Academy grounds. Live satellite feeds did not seem to show anything unusual. Romeo looked at the screen closely, he could see the old dormitory where he had stayed. He could not fight it, and again, his memories flooded his mind.

Romeo found himself in his room. The small dorm was shared by another boy his age. His nerves were unsteady as that boy had been taken to the detention room and had not returned for two days. The Academy was now a full blown prison. The tall fences surrounding the school seemed to make sense now. The young adults were all being treated like criminals in a labor camp as if they had committed heinous crimes. He had hoped Reaper and Aurora finished their plans for escape. But doubt still fogged his mind. Julia had told him to be strong and patient. It could be just a matter of time and the date of graduation would be soon enough. Then, they could just leave and start their new lives together. A black fog began to fill the memory. In his hands, he held up a photograph of Julia. The picture was taken on a set of stairs. She was looking at the camera with her cherry red cheeks and comforting smile. It was a picture she had given him a couple of years ago when they first started dating. It was the only one he carried.

Suddenly, a loud knocking rang at his door and the door swung open. Romeo stood at attention as two staff members entered the room. "Room search." The two members began tearing through the drawers of his night stand. Clothes flew in the air as the men dug around. The other lifted the mattress from his bed. Romeo stood still, the fear of disappearing in detention or the therapy treatment was fresh in his mind. Then another person walked into the room. It was the Provost. Romeo stood up straight as he feared the power that this man possessed and remained still.

"I'm here to make sure any distractions are confiscated. All personal items will be properly disposed of. We don't need anyone failing out of the Academy, now do we?" the Provost approached Romeo until they were face to face. "What's that in your hand?"

Romeo clutched onto the photo.

"Let me have it, now." the Provost ordered.

One of the staff raised a baton; fearing a beat down, Romeo reluctantly lifted his hand and opened it. The photo lay slightly crinkled on his palm.

The Provost grinned, "Thank you," he reached for the picture and took it with his fingers, "I appreciate your ability to comply. There is no need for fighting here." Provost held the photo up and recognized the girl in the photo. "You and this girl must be a couple, eh?" Provost pulled a small lighter out of his pocket. "This kind of thing can be a dangerous distraction." He held the lighter up to the photo in front of Romeo's eyes and lit it. The orange flame changed to green as the ink burned away on the photo. Within seconds the photo was ashes on the floor. Romeo remained still.

"This kind of thing can be hazardous to education." Provost stepped closer to him, "I don't want to see you two doing anything out of line, you hear?"

Romeo struggled to speak, filled with anger for the burning of his only picture. "Yes, sir." he said slowly. With that, the three left his room. He looked at the floor to see the small ash remains.

Romeo fell back into reality as Reaper called to him, "Romeo, don't you think? Hello?"

He shook his head to clear his mind. "Think about what?"

Reaper looked at him, "Are you okay? I've been talking to you the whole time about an approach. You'll be here on the east end by the old dormitories."

Romeo looked at the screen, "Yeah, I'll take care of it."

"Gothica and I will share the north side. We'll all meet back up in the cafeteria. Now that we have more freedom to move around the campus, we'll look at the administration building together so we don't miss anything." Reaper looked around and stopped at Crosshair, "And Crosshair, watch the courtyard."

The words echoed in Romeo's mind again. The courtyard was the central point of the Provost's demented assemblies. The one in particular made him drift into the black fog once again.

The students were all lined up and the Provost had something very important to discuss with the campus. 45 students filled the courtyard, his roommate was still missing. The microphone on the podium rang throughout the Academy walls.

The Provost's deep voice began to rattle Romeo's ears. "Good morning. I have called you all here to share a little something with you. As you may all have noticed, there are two young gentlemen up here who are looking slightly exhausted. Now, I'm sure everyone wants to know why these delinquents are up here and why you all get to see them. The fact of the matter is these two were found trying to escape. Digging a hole under the fence in the northeast corner of the campus. As it is obvious they were caught, these two will face severe punishment. All will witness. You all know that cheating can get you in the therapy room. Turns out, that trying to escape is a bit harsher. In fact, this has now made us step it up a notch in terms of security." A number of the staff walked onto the small stage with weapons in their hands. They were holding guns. "These are teargas, non-lethal firearms. With them comes a horrible stinging to the face and skin. Staff personnel have permission to use them when I deem it necessary." The two boys were taken to the front of the stage. "I do believe in second chances and a first time warning. So I will spare these two gentlemen. But let this be an example to you all. No one is allowed outside these fences and whoever attempts to, will not be so fortunate and action will be taken." The microphone shut off leaving with a loud screech.

"Romeo!"

Romeo rang out of his dream quickly and noticed the red lit cabin of the Ark once again. He panted heavily. The nightmare came to pass as the light at the cargo door turned yellow, it was almost time to land.

Reaper walked up to him and slapped his hand on his shoulder, "I know you don't want to be here. Believe me, it's not my first choice, either. But we need to focus."

Romeo took a deep breath, "Yeah, don't worry. I'll be good." he grinned. His hands grazed the side of his leg holster to ensure his M9 was present. The lights turned green, indicating it was time for drop off. He then moved to check his arms; the dagger was strapped tightly on his left arm. It, too, was returning to its place of origin.

Chapter 5

The night air was colder from when Romeo was here last. The Academy lay dormant after all these years. As far as he knew, not a soul would even want to be here. The Academy lay several miles from any town. The mesa it rested on was covered with white patches of snow and frost. Darkness filled the campus as it remained dormant and with no power. It was quiet and exceptionally eerie. Romeo took a breath as he stared at the dormitories. It was the first place to search for any clues. From there, it would be easy to sweep and meet back with the others in the cafeteria. He proceeded to the door but before he entered he looked back to see Crosshair make his way upon the roof of the administration building. Romeo's stomach curdled as the flashback overtook him.

Romeo observed the Academy under the night sky. The sounds of screams filled his ears. The rebellion of a handful of students had begun. Crosshair had been told to get on the roof and provide cover with the stolen tear gas gun. That way the others could make it to the rendezvous and escape. Romeo turned to see Julia's face filled with uncertainty and fear. His assurance was fading as Romeo felt himself fall back into reality. He watched

Crosshair scan the area and perch along the roof of the building. He turned towards the entryway and slowly entered.

The dark hallway was easy to navigate thanks to the Cat-Eye contact, made by Circuitcrusher a few years before. The long hallway led to multiple rooms that branched off. He stepped forward, detecting nothing unusual as he made his way deeper into the dorms. The silence was deafening. Romeo kept his senses on high alert, ready for any surprises. But the building just creaked from settling. His eyes scanned down the main hallway, it was dark and still. Not even the dust was moving.

The cold air inside allowed him to only see his breath. The long building was lifeless. In the quiet, he felt himself losing concentration. He gazed deeper down the hall until his eyes landed on what looked to be a shadow. It did not move, as if it was staring back at him. It did not appear to be anyone from the unit. His heart jumped and goosebumps filled his skin under his sneaking suit. The human like figure did not seem real. Petrified by who or even what it could be, Romeo whispered into his comms unit. "Anyone in the male dorms?"

"Negative." Reaper reported back.

"I'm with Reaper," Gothica followed.

"In the girl dorms." Violet radioed.

"On the roof of admin." Crosshair confirmed.

Romeo felt his nerves run cold as the figure remained still. Wondering if he was losing his mind, he stepped towards it. Then the figure seemed to hover towards him. In a flash, he drew his M9 pistol and watched as the figure moved to the left and into a dorm room. Romeo checked around, trying to gain control of his breath. The figure appeared to be gone. He stepped nervously towards the direction where the figure disappeared. Soon realizing where the figure dashed to, he felt dizzy. His mind took over as he approached his own dorm room.

Sunlight poured through the windows. Their first week at the Academy with Julia at his side, Romeo felt warmth and weightless. She wore a light red shirt as the two sat on the side of his bed. The bottom bunk. His roommate was still in class. Without a care in the world, he spoke to her. "I'm glad we both got accepted here." He held her close. "I was starting to lose hope."

"Me too, my love." Julia cheered. "We'll be able to have a great future now. A certificate of graduation."

Romeo smiled at her. "Yeah, it's pretty convenient this school accepted only orphan children. Guess we all get a second chance after dropping out of other schools. Once we're out of here, the sky is the limit."

She giggled at him, "I love seeing you this enthused." Julia embraced him tightly.

The old room slowly faded back to night and the warm embrace began to once again feel cold as Romeo stared at the ground. He could barely make out the blackened smudge from where the picture of Julia had burned to ash in front of him. Provost burned it to prove something. But all Romeo wanted was to strike him down for it. He broke from his trance and recalled seeing the shadow move to this room. But it was empty. No trace of anyone that had been there in years. The bunk bed remained there, covered in dust. He looked over to see the broken mirror of his nightstand against the wall. Then he backed out slowly into the hallway. It was time to finish his sweep and forget about this place.

Romeo proceeded out of the male dorms and followed the path that led straight to the cafeteria. He looked to see Crosshair still on the roof. Knowing he was covered, Romeo moved quickly to get to the rendezvous point with the others. As he opened the doors, the echo rang throughout the empty building. The sitting areas, booths and tables all remained. Some were moved and spilled over from the last night they were there. Romeo recalled the smell of lasagna. He quickly snapped out of it. Growing tired of his mind flashing back to the past, he pressed on to meet up with the others just ahead.

"Running a bit late?" Reaper observed him. "Everything okay?"

"Yeah," Romeo answered.

"Why did you ask about our locations?" Reaper pushed, "See anyone?"

Romeo shook his head, "No, just wanted to make sure I was checking the right place. You know it's still early, and I didn't finish my morning ritual, like sleeping."

"Oh, trust me," Gothica tapped his shoulder, "There's not enough beauty sleep in the world to fix this problem." She pointed at him.

"Okay, okay." Reaper smiled, "All that's left for us to do is check the admin building. Then we can get out of here."

Romeo agreed but his eyes caught sight of the kitchen. He looked down at his arm; the knife that Julia had found and given him remained fastened to its sheath. Violet noticed and tried to comfort him. "I know this place is hard to be in." Her voice brought little comfort to him. "But just know that...." Romeo proceeded towards the doors. He ignored the others. The doors swung open and it was back to the dreaded birthplace of the Cleansing Blade. He looked around to see nothing but a desolate wasteland engulfed by a winter's night. Then the corner of his eye caught a wisp of dust. It immediately sent him spiraling into that one particular night.

Romeo looked up to see the security guard's face bleeding from a slice. The dust that kicked up next to him had dissipated. Curiosity made him think of who might be around. And who had caused the wound. He turned to see Julia still hiding a few yards away. The force of the man's weight was easing up due to his wound. Romeo pushed him off and stood up. His thoughts then seemed to flash as he heard the horrid scream come from her. She landed on top of him, the dagger in his hand. Her blood spilling upon his clothes. He held her tightly as her dying breath told him "live". He had kissed her forehead as the last tear he had shed ran slowly down his cheek.

He snapped out of his memory. Feeling a hand gently touch his shoulder. Reaper spoke, "I think we need to keep moving. Let's get out of here." Romeo remained unmoved. He looked up at the light pole that stood next to the spot. Still broken. The brown and gray wall had some black spots towards the ground. Her blood still stained the walls. It remained there after all these years. Then a strange feeling overtook him. He could not control his tongue. "She died here." He pointed with his chin, "Right there."

Reaper looked over at Violet who wiped her eyes from approaching tears, "Yeah, I know." Reaper nodded. "It wasn't in vain."

Violet tried to comfort him, "It wasn't your fault. The guard made a mistake." It was difficult for her to speak.

"You know what's funny." Romeo mumbled, "After all these years, you all still don't know."

Reaper squinted in interest, "What do you mean?"

Romeo pulled the dagger from its sheath. He raised it to his face. The word "LIVE" next to the handle. "I promised her I would take care of her. But all I could promise is that me, I, would live."

"You can't carry that guilt." Violet tried assuring.

Romeo gazed at the blade. "All these years have passed. I never thought this day would come."

Reaper remained silent and watched as Romeo focused on the blade. He was not normally willing to speak so openly. It was strange that he would spill himself in front of them. Maybe the Academy had broken him. Romeo took a breath, "To finally see the guilty person."

"What are you talking about?" Violet's face had tear trails running down it.

Romeo closed his eyes in regret, "I am responsible." The words that escaped him rattled the others. Relief briefly filled him.

"How could you say that?" Violet kept trying, "How…"

"Violet," Reaper shook his head to keep silent.

He gripped the dagger tightly. As if choking it into submission. Romeo knew what was about to come out of his mouth. He stared at the dagger. Julia had fallen onto it while he held it. She died because of him. But the team had no idea. They never knew. But now was not the time to throw them off of the objective. He sheathed the blade. No tears in his eyes. No urge to grieve. "Provost had no regard for the loss. Her blood is on his hands as much as it is on mine."

Reaper was careful to not trigger any unwanted emotions in him, "But she would be proud of what you've become."

Romeo turned to look at him, "Are you sure about that?"

"We need to check the admin building." Reaper turned around, "Let's go."

Romeo looked past Reaper to see Crosshair standing on the roof observing them. His goggles removed from his head. He knew he had heard. He turned to look at Violet caressing her hair with one hand and wiping her eyes with the other. He felt the need to speak. "She admired you a lot."

She sniffled, "Thanks,"

The team split up and moved towards the administration building. Gothica caught up with Reaper. "Are you even expecting to find anything here?"

"With the way things are going right now." Reaper looked back at her, "I'm afraid to uncover more."

Chapter 6

The administration building was quiet and empty. The winter air had filled the room. Old computer consoles had been locked away inside. It took little effort for Gothica to pick the locks that sealed up the large building. Reaper was close behind her and the others closed in the gap. They were in uncharted territory in a familiar place. No working lights added with the dim star-filled sky, made it difficult to see inside. Too many dark corners filled the room.

Romeo felt himself easing back into the mission. After nearly spilling the truth had had an unusual relief to it. The memory of Julia did not feel any better. And the silence that filled the large office area gave his mind no ease. There was no sign of any life inside. Nothing but the cold chill of winter air. The team spread out, searching for any clues as to Provost's whereabouts. Romeo gazed at a large poster with webs and dust shielding it. The words could still be made out; "The Academy, Futures with Promise."

Romeo grinded his teeth, as if the poster was mocking him. He looked throughout the empty room and spotted Reaper looking for any clues within the desks. Romeo's attention then diverted to a figure standing behind him. Like the one he remembered seeing in the dorms. He shook his head to snap out of it and called out. "Reaper, behind you."

Reaper looked behind him, only to see nothing there. "What?"

Romeo did not see anything. "What the hell?" He mumbled to himself. "I thought I saw something."

Reaper shook his head and looked around the room. Then his eye caught a few symbols on the wall behind him. "At this?" He asked as he looked back at Romeo. "Symbols of some kind."

Romeo walked towards it, it was where he saw the figure, the ghost. Oracle's words echoed in his head as he recalled her saying something about a ghost. It was probably a coincidence since he was unsure about her ability, and only telling Reaper what he wanted to hear. Romeo had trust issues, and she was still too new to be trusted.

"Looks like the letter P and versus symbol and then this." Gothica analyzed it more. "I think it's an R. It's been written in the dust, could be a day or so old. If not today."

"P vs R?" Reaper searched for more clues. Reaper recalled the signature, "That P looks like the way Provost signed his letter. Finally, something."

Romeo moved up to view the markings. "Provost vs....who?"

Gothica moved her hand across the wall, "Whoever R is."

"Very vague clue if you ask me." Romeo chimed in.

"Guess now we just need to find more markings." Violet sounded enthused. "Like a treasure hunt."

"I really don't care to find any here." Romeo snickered.

Reaper looked around, "Spread out and scan the walls. Doorways, anything. He wants us to play in a scavenger hunt."

Romeo walked to check the far corner. The others were very quiet, making it easy to pick up on the sound of the gentle breeze making its way through the doorway. Just dirt and cobwebs filled the corners and faces of the walls. Romeo had his doubts, and the way to the detention room was on the other side of the building, which they still needed to check out. Romeo found nothing as he scanned for more marks. He looked over at the others to see if they had made progress. Violet moved carefully, not making a sound. He observed her as she checked towards the ceiling. The Cat-Eye was working extra hard to make the room manageable to see at a distance. He looked up to where she was gazing, then looked back. In the corner of his eye, he noticed something stand and hover towards her. A shadow floated at her. He could not believe his hallucinations; it seemed to move as if defying gravity!

"Violet, get down!" Romeo drew his pistol.

She turned to him and noticed he was ready to fire. She noticed the angle of his weapon and turned around. But nothing was behind her. Romeo took a deep breath and saw nothing.

"What the hell is wrong with you?" Reaper asked, sounding agitated.

Romeo shook his head, scanning nearby for anything. "Nothing, I need air." He turned to Reaper and saw the shadowy figure behind him. "There!" Romeo aimed only to notice the figure had disappeared.

Reaper looked around. Still with a calm but agitated voice, "What is the problem, Romeo?"

Romeo tried to catch his breath. "I need air. I'm seeing things."

Gothica spoke up, "I think I found something."

"What is it?" Reaper was sidetracked.

She continued, "There's a door in here."

Reaper walked hastily towards her position, "Where?"

"Tucked away behind this shelf. Even has a security key pad. Looks like it's still functioning." Gothica drew her crossbow pistol.

"How do you know?" Romeo moved to her location.

"The keys are still lit up." Gothica said.

"Great work," Reaper scrambled to her location. "Anyone got a clue as to what the code might be?"

Gothica looked around, she peered to the wall where the letters were written. "I think I'll take a shot in the dark." She reached for the pad and punched in the letters, P V S R.

The door shot opened, startling the team. Reaper drew his hi-cap pistol.

"Guess we can look here," Gothica raised her crossbow pistol. "After you."

He took a second to reach Crosshair on comms, "Crosshair, we've found something. Proceeding deeper into the basement of admin. Keep a close eye on the area. Just in case."

"You got it." Crosshair gave his reassuring reply.

Reaper nodded to the others and proceeded first. The narrow stairs made it difficult to navigate freely. A dim light appeared at the bottom indicating a possibility that someone was still there. Reaper crept slower. It sounded as if someone was typing. His nerves were on edge. Dealing with Romeo's freak out and the possibility of Provost being around the corner made him stop for a second. He took a deep breath to regain his composure. If Provost was here, what would Romeo try to do? Reaper snapped back into the mission and was ready identify the person in the room below.

His hi-cap was the first to turn the corner, then he peeked into the room. There seemed to be large amounts of research and medical equipment scattered throughout the area. There was no sign of the noise, however. Reaper turned to Gothica and signaled her to follow him. He looked up to signal Romeo and Violet to take the opposite side. With a nod, the four quickly ran down the steps and secured the room. With confirmations from each to indicate no threats, Reaper looked around to notice another cutaway. Two doors, one was open, and the noise was coming from in there. He dashed silently to the edge of the wall. The others stacked behind him. Romeo pulled his dagger out and rested his gun hand on top of his knife hand. He was ready for whatever lay inside the room. Reaper wasted no time; he turned the corner and found himself staring at a suddenly cowering man.

"Freeze!" Reaper held his pistol steadily at the man. "Identify yourself."

The whimpering man crawled back into the corner and held his legs. "Wha?! What? I'm a geneticist. Dr. Howard Hampton."

Romeo burst through the door past Reaper, "Where is he?" He demanded.

"Who? I don't know what you're talking about." the man trembled.

Romeo stepped forward but was grabbed by Reaper as he pressured the man, "Where is he?"

"Please, I don't know what's going on."

Gothica approached the man, "Philip Johnson. Is he here?"

"I, I," The man struggled, "I work for him yes."

Romeo tried to get closer but Reaper kept a solid hold, "Stand down." Reaper ordered. "He's not here."

Romeo was not satisfied. He turned to notice Violet looking at him nervously. "We'll keep looking." She said. Romeo shook his head as Reaper loosened his grip on his arm. He felt let down and walked out of the room.

Gothica continued to interrogate the man, "Was he here recently?"

"Uh...Yes," the man's breath was shallow, "Yes, he was here a week ago. Wanted me to continue working on the last of the data on the genome."

"What genome?" Gothica held her hand out and pulled the man up. "What's going on here?"

The doctor fixed his glasses. "The genome research he was conducting here."

Reaper shook his head in disappointment. He knew it. Provost had been busy, hiding a secret from them. "What kind of research, doctor?" He observed the man. Tall, at least six feet. Younger, mid 30's. Dark blonde hair and glasses covering what appeared to be hazel eyes. For a doctor, he appeared to be in good shape. "What's Philip been conducting here?"

"I'm...I'm sorry," The man fidgeted, "Who are you people?"

Gothica remained calm, "Old colleagues of his. Trying to touch base with him."

"Um, strange way to greet colleagues." The doctor fixed his shirt. "We've been working on a genetics Enhancer Solution. Something he took very seriously." the man observed them. "Did he conduct business elsewhere? I knew he was a busy man."

"He was." Reaper said, "Very busy apparently, what's in the other room?"

"Uh, I don't think you have authorization." The man wiped his forehead.

"I think we do." Reaper spoke firmly. "Now show us."

"Okay, okay...please, just don't hurt me." the man walked towards the entrance and froze at the door. Romeo's piercing eyes made him shake nervously.

"Let's move, Dr. Hampton." Reaper nudged the man forward.

They moved to the locked door on the adjacent wall. The doctor input the code and the door pushed opened. They all moved into the room. In front of them were three tube-like chambers. Reaper scanned the room. More computers and medical equipment littered the walls and surrounded the chambers.

"What the hell are these?" Reaper demanded.

"Uh, they are vitality chambers for the subjects." the man moved to the side. "Are you all the new patients?"

"Patients?" Gothica asked.

The man fixed his glasses. "Uh, there were three patients that we were conducting the Enhancer Solution on."

"You were experimenting on people?" Violet sounded disgusted.

"They were volunteers, soldiers from various agencies. Philip wanted to conduct genetic enhancement on them." The doctor stood ashamed.

"He was testing it and then he was going to use it on us." Reaper clicked his tongue, growing more and more impatient. "Just three? Where are they?" Reaper turned to look over at Romeo who stood quiet in the corner. He knew the night had been rough, but now things were getting worse.

"Philip transported the two surviving subjects." the man continued, "They were in bad shape, however; both near death."

"So where's the one that did die?" Gothica examined the empty chambers.

"We dispose of them properly. He was cremated." The man rubbed his hands.

Gothica looked over at him, "Why so forth telling with all of this?"

The man looked at Reaper and Romeo in the background, "Do I have much choice?"

Reaper proceeded with more questions, "Did he keep any records here?"

"Yes," The doctor stuttered nervously, "As I said before, I was working here on the data collection from the last trial. I assume you're gonna need it?" The doctor's eyes grew as he saw Romeo pull his dagger out. "Of course, sorry."

"You have ten minutes, then you're coming with us." Reaper said.

The man became nervous again, "Uh, where are we going?"

Romeo turned to exit, "Away from this place."

Chapter 7

The Ark was on root back to the Nest. The ride was surprisingly comfortable for all of them. Knowing that the Academy was now long gone, they could all focus on the doctor being transported with them. Reaper paced around, observing the sleeping doctor.

"Are you sure about this?" Gothica said cautiously as she approached him, "Bringing him with us is taking a big risk."

Reaper was comforted in her concern. "We took you didn't we?"

Gothica smiled for a second, "Yes, but this is different."

"We'll keep him locked in one of the empty bedrooms." Reaper looked over at her. "We need him. As of right now, he is our only lead to finding Provost. And God only knows what he's doing."

"I understand that," she insisted, "But like I said, the data he took from there can give us something instead of having the baggage."

"We've spent over a year looking for him." Reaper looked at her, "And desperation calls for a change of tactics. Especially when we get a lucky break like this."

"Understood," She felt defeated, but at the same time could see he was growing. "Your judgment is getting better." She winked at him. "We'll just keep a close watch on him then." She noticed Reaper looked tired, "Happy to be out of there?"

He smirked at her, "You have no idea."

"I think I got the gist of it." She waved her hand towards Romeo.

Reaper shuddered at his thoughts as they flashed over to the Academy, "Provost had set that whole thing up just waiting for us to make a move. And little did we know he actually wanted us to."

Gothica observed him, "Look at it this way, how many lives have you saved now because of what you've become since then?" she pointed at him, as if showing him what he had become.

"Right," Reaper looked down at himself, "That place created us in a sense."

"It's your home?" Gothica teased, "Not sure if it's a happy one."

"Unlike yours?"

"Compared to that? Definitely. My home wasn't all that bad. I do find myself missing it from time to time, though." Gothica caught herself daydreaming about it, she smiled at him. He noticed something in her eyes said it all. The guilt he carried for all of the non-original Cleansing Blade members was heavy at times. They still had lives to go back to. They did not come from that Academy.

Reaper could tell the subject was fragile. It was time to go back to the mission at hand. "I guess we can be grateful Provost hasn't had the opportunity to test the Enhancer Solution on us."

"He's probably been trying to perfect it, after we all accepted the Adrenaline Solution so well, it was time to improve on that." She analyzed, "But it sounds like the subjects keep dying. You think he'll be after us to test us?"

"It's not like we'll be warm and inviting if we see him again. So I doubt he'll try to get too close for now."

Her cautious voice took hold again, "I hope so. But what about the doctor?"

Reaper thought about him, and Provost being as careful as he was. "Let's hope he's not in on it. After all, he did work under orders from Provost himself." Reaper assured.

Gothica looked over at Romeo who was staring up at the lights of the cabin. "What about him? He started to lose it back there."

"Stress, hallucinations of Julia probably." Reaper spoke quietly. "I think he uncovered more than he wanted."

"We should assess him once we're back at the Nest." She recommended. "I think he's unfit for combat at the moment. He could be a liability next time he sees action."

"He may be unstable, but know that he won't let you down when a situation gets out of hand." he argued, "He'll be fine. We'll brief everyone once we get back."

"Got it," Gothica tipped her head, "Way to stay cool out there. Thought you were going to change things on us once we landed."

He chuckled a little, "I've been working on it. Can't you tell?"

"Yeah, I'm proud of you." Gothica patted his arm. She looked behind him to see Crosshair looking eager to speak up and nodded to him.

"Hey uh, I have something to tell you." the sniper stepped to join the two standing alongside the consoles in the cabin. "Reaper, I uh, have a confession to make."

Reaper looked up at him curiously, "What's bothering you?"

"You trust me right?" Crosshair wiped his dirty forehead. The rim of the goggles on his head made an obvious indentation on his hair.

Reaper crossed his arms, waiting for another hammering story from one of his teammates. "What is it, Crosshair?"

He took a deep breath, "Listen, I've been doing the recon assignments you've instructed, but some of the locations I reported were, bogus. I've found myself reminiscing of my past life. You know, before all of this."

"And?"

"And…..I've been spying on my father." Crosshair said, hiding his embarrassment, "I found out where he was. After all these years he looks the same."

Reaper was alarmed. "I thought he was dead?"

"I remember when I was a kid, he would take me with him on long drives to look at animals in the wild. Then one day he left. Not sure why, but I assumed he was dead. Until just recently."

Reaper could hear the shame in his voice, "Crosshair, I, I don't know what to say. You've been using the Ark to spy on your father?"

"It was the locations. One of them was close to a town he lives in. Asked Gothica and Motherboard for a little help. Then I redirected the Ark to make a stop there on occasion." He looked at Reaper with shame, "I know, I've messed up."

"Messed up?" Gothica butted in, "You have a family."

Reaper tried to direct the conversation, "Crosshair, why didn't you say anything before?"

He bowed his head, "I figured it would be against protocol, you know."

"So, I assume you're thinking about seeing him in person?" Reaper was unsure how to feel.

The tall sniper looked at him with hope, "Yeah,"

"Crosshair, I can't have you just running around society. Look at you. You're a trained killer with little interaction with real people outside of the Cleansing Bl…." Reaper caught himself, "The Shadows of the Sun. You can't just leave and expect to be, uh, normal."

Gothica looked at Reaper with a condescending look, "Just because he's Crosshair to us, doesn't mean he's not a real person."

Reaper turned back at Crosshair, "Look, you're us. We are a unit. We haven't had a normal life in over six years."

"We still had lives before that." Crosshair replied.

Reaper struggled to speak. He looked at Gothica who was more understanding and seemed enthralled by Crosshair's life. She asked him, "Crosshair, I think that's a great idea, but don't you think your timing is a bit off?"

"Yeah, I can see that." He said, "But it's been running around my mind every waking moment. I can't get over it. I want to try again. If not just to say hello to him."

Reaper looked at her and figured she had something to do with it. "You knew?"

"I've got more experience in this department, not to mention you're really not approachable when it comes to asking for vacation time." She grinned.

Reaper bit his lip in reluctance. He looked at Gothica who obviously was more supportive of the team's needs. He gave her a wave, "Make the call."

She looked surprised, "Okay, Crosshair, as of now your new mission is to gather intel on well, yourself. You can have a week to do so."

Crosshair's eyes filled with joy, he smiled at both of them, "Thank you. I promise to be back on time."

Reaper shook his head, but could not help but feel the enthusiasm. "Good luck, Crosshair. I hope you find what you're looking for."

"Thank you, Reaper," he smiled, "I promise to be back and ready for action in seven days."

"Sounds great," Reaper instructed, "We'll set down at the Nest, get your stuff and go where you need to. It will take us some time to get more information on Provost, anyway." Reaper turned to look at the others watching from the bench in front of the lockers. "This never leaves the Ark."

Finally back at the Nest, Romeo stood still as the hot water from the shower rained down on his body. He found himself fading in the steam. His memories were starting to control him. Never had they reached this point. His head found its way to the last night at the Academy. The campus was silent and the students had all been rounded up and forced back into their rooms. All but seven of them. Romeo took his time to walk towards the others. The quiet night air of the courtyard was filled with the glow of the functioning light posts. They appeared to be working fine after the other kid, Circuitcrusher, had disabled them. To his left, Boss; the gray haired man that helped him with large guard. It was him that had cut the guard's face and allowed Romeo the upper hand. Then to the right, his stomach ached with nerves. Provost stood before them all. And the words that came from his mouth would forever be remembered, "Ah Romeo, Romeo. Why thou art?" Provost spoke. "He was born in tragedy. And you, Romeo, will be rebirthed by this place. You passed the test to be one with the elite." Romeo stood fighting back the tears. He could not understand what was happening. It was all a test, a game. Provost had made sure they rebelled so he could select them to join his Cleansing Blade.

"Thanks to the Reaper here," Provost moved on to naming the next one. "The man who reaped the team together and planned this little escapade. I must say, I'm happy you stepped up." He looked over at the next one on the team, "Then you have this young man" Provost observed the tall young man that had repelled some of the guards using their own weapons from the roof. "It takes guts to be responsible from a distance and still effective, Crosshair. That is your new name."

Romeo could see the others. Violet just stared at his shirt, covered in blood, Julia's blood. She too had been injured. A gash across her arm and a little one across her cheek showed an unusual color of blood. It was purple. Provost's voice resonated, "Ah, my sweet Violet, dry your tears. For you have started the new adventure of your life. And you get to help others, which I know you like to do."

Provost continued as the giant approached him, "Monster out of the darkness. Boss, I still can't believe this kid held back the four biggest staff we had here. Impressive." He looked over at the tall pale bookworm, "And you, I am really impressed with how you disabled the power here for a few moments for Crosshair to take the weapons and start the riot. Good at electronics."

"The ol' Circuitcrusher here." Monster laughed and smacked him on the back.

Provost smiled, "I like that, Circuitcrusher. Has a ring to it."

Romeo looked over at the last remaining true member of Cleansing Blade. She stood directly under the light post. It was due to her knowledge of the staff's patrols that they were able to anticipate them and make their move. An aura sat on her head from the light above her.

"You, pretty girl," Provost smiled, "You took charge and outsmarted a few of my staff. I think I'll call you…"

"Aurora," Reaper called out, "Call her, Aurora."

Provost smiled, "Done, I like that. Welcome to the Cleansing Blade."

Romeo shut the water off and walked out of a refreshing hot shower. He wiped the fog from the mirror to see himself while he shaved. The thoughts of the cold Academy lingered as he stroked his chin. Memories of Julia were becoming unavoidable. But strangely, returning to the sight of her death was soothing. As if closure was finally starting to set in. He grabbed his electronic shaver and turned to see his left cheek. He gently ran the humming blades across the small amount of five o'clock shadow that was starting to appear. His thoughts dwelled yet again into that fateful night. If Julia had survived, what would her new name have been?

"Promise me…." Julia struggled.

"Yes, what?" Romeo fought the grief.

"You….will live."

Romeo would forever remember those words. His dagger had the word engraved on it. As a reminder of his promise to her. And this promise, he would not break. Comforted by his determination, he grinned and adjusted his face again to check his right cheek. Then he noticed a small cut on the lower part of his neck. Alarmed, he bent forward to see it clearly. It was the symbol P he had seen on the wall at the Academy.

Chapter 8

Meanwhile the rest of the team was barely starting the day. Violet quickly made it to the rooms in time to catch Amraam getting out of the shower. After the events during the assignment in the Academy, she was emotionally drained. The reminiscing of that time in her life was anything but pleasant. Romeo's revelation was hard to wrap her mind around. Him, feeling so guilty, practically saying that he had killed Julia made her uneasy. Violet could feel her stomach curdle with the thought. She loved Julia. She was a sweet and kind young girl that only wanted a brighter future. But all of that was gone. Romeo blamed himself and seemed to have made that impossible. Provost had ultimately made it impossible for any of them. She struggled to fight against the negative thoughts that were flooding her mind.

Violet dashed down the hallway faster, wiping her face from falling tears. With Crosshair now given permission to pursue his once "real" life made her think hard about hers. Her memories of her childhood were foggy. The hallway lights seemed to trigger an old memory of her mother and father. She vaguely remembered the car and sitting in the back seat. She could see her father driving and her mother talking to him. Her lush blond hair waving in the wind, then black. Only the sight of broken glass littered the interior seats. She could feel her heart sink faster into sadness as she pulled herself out of the old memory. She was desperate to maintain control. Then her hopes reentered her mind as Amraam made it out of the showers and back into the hallway.

Violet leapt at him, catching him off guard.

"Did you miss me or what?" he wrapped his arms around her. Without his favorite bandana on his head, it left him feeling somewhat exposed as the short black hair on his head stood straight up.

She embraced him tightly but kept silent.

"You okay?" Amraam held her, "Where have you been?" He waited till she regained her composure.

"Reaper wanted us on assignment, it was urgent." Violet felt his hand wipe away another tear that ran down her cheek.

Amraam grew concerned. "Is everything okay? What happened?"

Violet sniffled, "It's okay. Nothing bad. Just, going back there, to the Academy, brought up too many horrible memories."

Amraam pulled her in for another embrace. "It's okay, I know. It was bad place back then. But today is new day. It'll be alright."

"I know it will." Violet held him as tight as she could.

Amraam was in slight shock. Violet was crumbling before him. Something she never did. Normally she was the one to bring spirits up from dark times. But this time, she seemed frightened. It put him at alert. "I guess that means we're briefing in a few then, huh?"

"Yeah," Violet said, looking tired.

Amraam pulled her in and rubbed his nose along the back of her neck. Her finely braided pony tail tickled his cheek. Then his nose moved over a rough patch of skin. He opened his eyes and noticed her blood was dried up on the back of her neck. He looked closer and noticed what appeared to be a purple scab. "Did you guys see any combat there?"

Violet opened her eyes and looked up at him shaking her head. "No, nobody but a doctor we took in for questioning."

Amraam nodded, "Hmph, sounds exciting. You have a scratch back here." He turned her around and moved her blond braid to see the scratch. It looked to be the letter, P.

Reaper and Gothica had just finished taking the unconscious doctor to his room and sealed the door. It was going to be a little while before Reaper would be ready for a briefing. Time to unwind. The jolt from being at the Academy had him feeling a bit drained. First thing was first, it was time to let Boss know then reinitiate the hunt for Provost. He watched Gothica leave to her room. Her wisdom was indispensable to him. Her mentorship allowed him to adapt as their leader. And now with Provost missing, her help along with Boss's was greatly appreciated. Her more caring and easy going attitude allowed him to see things differently instead of judging everything by the book. Crosshair leaving to revisit what could be a window to his past, his family, was a bit unusual. Then again, nothing this night had been normal. Crosshair was ever reliable. He was always faithful and there to do his job. And he was the best at it. What would he find after all these years about his father? What would he learn? What about the others that had lives before they accepted the Cleansing Blade? Reaper shook out of it and looked down the hallway towards Boss's quarters. He needed to bring him up to speed on the situation. It would have been easy to follow the scent of a burning cigarette, but the Nest had state of the art air filtration.

Reaper proceeded down the hallway thinking of how to approach Boss with the situation, but that would have to wait. His eyes caught another pair. The marble filled eyes of Oracle made him nervous. Entranced, he struggled to break away, but her freshly bathed body made it difficult. Knowing she could read his mind he tried to think of something fast. He struggled to swallow as she wore nothing but a lean sports top and underwear. "Oracle, good, good morning." he moved his mouth quickly, "We're back from the mission. It'll be a few moments to get everyone down here to brief soon."

Oracle seemed to look past him, through him, "I see you brought something with you."

Reaper smiled, she was good, "Yeah, Dr. Hampton, a geneticist, is locked in the empty room upstairs. We knocked him out to get him here. We'll have to wake him up before we question him later."

Oracle tilted her head as if examining him, "Hampton." She mumbled. She looked back at Reaper, "Are you okay?"

Reaper worried she was reading his thoughts about her, "Uh, yeah." His mind went back to the Academy to try and throw her ability, "It was cold there. And too many memories…"

"Did you find the ghost?" she asked.

Reaper shook his head, "More like a skeleton hiding in Romeo's closet." He watched her as she approached him. His heart beat sped up. Through his gloves, he could feel his palms sweat.

"There is more. Something you brought back, and something you let go." Oracle raised her hand to his cheek.

Reaper stood for a second. As if savoring the soft touch of her palm, but then spoke quickly, "Yeah, uh, yeah, Crosshair too. He needed to find closure in other places. So, I let him go, to make contact with his father."

Oracle smiled, "That's not like you. Aurora would be pleased."

Reaper's mind flashed to Aurora for a brief second. Her strong role as second in command made him work twice as hard to please her. She would ensure he was acting as leader fairly, instead of like an annoying parent. Hearing that made him happy to know that maybe Aurora would have been proud. His thoughts slowly dissolved once he felt Oracle's palm leave his face. He found himself staring eye to eye with her standing closer to him. He could feel himself thinking about it. About his lips meeting hers. The urge was great, and he knew she would find that out soon. It was time to divert to escape her psychic grasp.

"I need to speak with Boss," he said and stepped back as Oracle seemed to be frozen in place. She stood up straight and appeared to be looking for something. "Do you need help getting back to your room?"

Oracle paused, then looked directly at him, "No, I can manage. Thank you."

Reaper proceeded down the hallway to meet with Boss before the rest of the team was ready. He cleared his mind from the strong feelings he was developing for Oracle. Something about her made his blood run warm. It was hard for him to fathom. Could he really be falling for her? Just as his mind raced to find an answer, Boss emerged from his quarters. Pleased, and somewhat relieved, Reaper sped up to meet him. "Boss, we have a lead."

"I know," Boss opened a fresh pack of smokes from his pocket. "Oracle filled me in on what you guys did."

"Oh," Reaper's momentum was slowed. Oracle had told him what happened. Could she have known what they saw? "Well, good. We made it back, but I sent Crosshair to check on another lead. We have someone here for questioning as well, a Dr. Hampton that worked under Provost on something, bad."

"Good to hear the trail is fresh again." Boss's lighter clicked and a large cloud of smoke escaped his mouth. The flame lit up his face, his blue eyes and silver hair reflected the ember of the cigarette. "Well done, Reaper. Now what is this something?"

Reaper proceeded, "Apparently Provost has been working on some kind of new solution, called Enhancer Solution, something he needed geneticists for. Dr. Hampton ran a testing trial on three volunteers that we know of, and that as far as we know, are dead. Provost was moving the trial elsewhere."

Boss showed a little concern. Weakness or worry could never be exposed. A lesson he had taught them back in training. Not to expose yourself to your enemy. "I trust you brought more than just that doctor in for questioning?"

"Yes, we have all of the data they collected from the project. Boss, it was being done at the Academy."

"I heard you went back there. Glad you could muster up the will to do so." Boss took another puff. "And I'm sure you found the labs in the basement?"

Reaper looked at him peculiarly, "Yeah, as a matter of fact, we did."

Boss took a deep puff, "You remember what I told you about truth? That it's a deadly weapon that can also cleanse us?" Boss was at his best with ancient wisdom.

Reaper felt weak, "Yes, sir. You know about something in the labs?"

Boss nodded, "We had developed the Adrenaline Solution there. That's why the exercise was done at that campus."

Reaper stopped breathing for a second to try and wrap his head around yet another revelation. "What?" he whispered.

Boss continued, "And why the select few were chosen. The immunizations you all received before enrolling were a small refined dose of it." Reaper was in a state of denial. After all this time, Boss finally exposed the truth behind the Academy. Boss was puffing on his cigarette as he spoke, "I'm sorry to have to tell you. You never were to find out as long as Provost was here, but since he's not, it's time you heard the truth." Boss was direct.

"I've had enough truth for one night." Reaper thought about Romeo and Crosshair. "I don't want to hear anymore."

"The truth is always more violent to cope with than even death." Boss's wisdom and age was starting to show. "He and I constructed and planned the Academy for years before we actually sent off and accepted new students. You know how the rest goes." Reaper remained speechless. Boss puffed from his cigarette, "Knowing that now, it makes sense that Philip would try to use that old facility. Makes sense that Oracle helped you come to that conclusion too. She is great recruit from that military research center." Boss could tell that Reaper was still wrapping matters around his head. "Listen, you are a great leader and your ruling to recruit and initiate are improving greatly. I know because you showed that at the Academy. I made sure you were more closely followed and chosen for the project."

Reaper was surprised to hear Boss spill the truth. It was not like him to talk so much about it. Let alone talk much at all. He knew Boss had watched over them at the Academy. And since Provost's disappearance, Boss remained with them, supporting them every step of the way. Provost too supported and kept a close I on them back then. Reaper thought about his ex-leader, "But why was HE so cold to the death of one student?" Reaper had to know. Since it was a night of revelations, Julia's death had been bothering him as Romeo had pointed out the location of her death.

Boss finished his smoke and shook his head, "Casualties in the field cannot be dwelled into. And from that point in your lives, moving forward quickly was the best way to mold you. You above all should understand the sacrifices we've made."

Reaper understood what he was doing. Moving towards the future and burying the past quickly was a necessity for survival in their line of work. It may have been the best way, but was it the right way? Even with his devotion to Boss and his team, Reaper was still learning on his own. Boss was right about them moving on quickly, but he did not see Romeo freaking out at the Academy either. And the well-being of his team weighed heavy upon him daily. But it was time to move forwards with the conversation, "Boss, I just want to start on Provost's trail again." Reaper spoke softly, as if fighting the urge to scream. "This doctor needs to be questioned and the data analyzed. If Provost is going to test this stuff on more people, then it looks like we're going to have more victims." He remembered Gothica's idea, "Or he's coming for us to test it."

"Not even he would be that foolish." Boss insisted.

"Maybe the doctor's bait?"

Boss rubbed his gray haired chin, "Perhaps. We'll need to keep a close eye on him. In case Provost injected him with some kind of possible way to spread it. Try not to touch him or share anything with him." Boss looked at Reaper, "We'll need to keep him alone and in a secure place while he's here."

"Don't worry," He nodded, "He's locked in one of the most air filtered rooms in the Nest." Reaper turned to notice Gothica approaching. She appeared to have had a haircut. "What the…"

Gothica smiled as her freshly cut hair fell just past her ears and seemed to reach her neck towards the back. "Don't like my new hair cut?"

Reaper grinned at the shorter cut. "Looks good. Why'd you cut it?"

"I just got tired of dealing with the swaying long hair always tied back. This shorter hair is way more manageable. It took me nearly ten years just to grow it out that long before." Gothica smiled. "Figured since it's a day of moving on, I can return to my natural look instead of my fake, dyed look." She ran her fingers through her hair. The light brown hair now mostly dominated the dark red it once was.

Boss nodded, "Looks great, Gothica. You did it yourself?"

"Yeah, not too bad eh?" She spun around to show them her fine work at trimming hair.

Reaper shook his head. Pleasantly amazed of how good she worked on her own hair, then laughed as his eyes found a scratch on the back of her neck. "You seemed to cut yourself back there."

Gothica squinted in surprised, "No I didn't. I'm perfectly capable of knowing what hair and skin feels like."

Reaper laughed, "I trust you. But you did, look." He walked up to her and turned her around as if to show her. Then his look shifted to confusion. It was a small slice mark that resembled the letter P. "What the hell?"

Boss walked up to both of them and threw his cigarette on the ground. "I think you both have seen the same barber." He said as he noticed the same mark on the back of Reaper's neck.

Chapter 9

The briefing room was quiet until Reaper broke the silence. A hologram photo of Provost stood above the center console. The team all looked around at Romeo, Gothica, and Violet who stood next to him. Reaper grew impatient. "Romeo, what did you see out there?"

"This isn't going to get us anywhere," Romeo argued, "It was nothing. Just my mind freaking me out."

"Obviously not," Gothica spoke up, "We are all marked."

Romeo shook his head. He did not want to believe it.

Oracle walked forward as if she sensed something. "A ghost."

Romeo grew frustrated, "Dream Girl here won't let up will she?" He wanted to say more, but starting an argument would get them nowhere either. So he stopped while he was ahead.

Gothica tried connecting the clues in her head. "Someone else had to have been there. Someone with the same skill as us."

"Provost." Reaper struggled to accept the words he spoke. "He was there. The P, Provost was right behind us. Taunting us."

"If that's the case, why didn't he kill us?" Romeo asked.

Gothica cut in, "I think the question we need to ask is, why he led us to the lab?"

Reaper acknowledged the question, "Right, why did Provost lead us to find out about his new project? He obviously wanted us to."

Oracle spoke up again, "His name must be looked at from another perspective. Then you will find the ghost."

"Are we still on this?!" Romeo grew agitated with her. "Drop it Dream Girl!"

"Hey!" Reaper defended, "That's enough." Everyone kept quiet for second. "Listen, we need to collect ourselves and begin accessing the data that we collected. Then formulate a strategy on how to get this doctor to work with us and find out where Provost's next stop is. That's all. Everybody dismissed except for you three." Reaper pointed to Motherboard, Radical and Circuitcrusher who all stepped forward towards him. "I trust you guys are finally finished with that CIA database and the drones?" Reaper had sent them on missions to clean Radical's previous CIA slate. Since the SG-205 drone, dubbed Linda, had discovered him, it was a high priority to wipe Radical's life clean from any government database. And these three had pulled through.

Radical nodded, "Of course. As I say, any problem can be fixed with the right amount of explosives."

"That's what you said about the CIA data housing center. And look what happened that time?" Motherboard criticized.

Reaper looked over at him, "You what?"

"No, relax." Radical shrugged it off. "Not exactly. Look, I didn't have time to reach into the file, she talked me out of the, blowing it up part, so I compromised, and burned it down instead. Just my section though. With the cannon bombs."

Circue could not resist and butt in, "I knew you would like them. And not to worry, Reaper, I designed them to only blow out in a certain direction. A controlled explosion."

Motherboard shook her head, "I had nothing to do with it. Other than it did look like an accident, sort of."

"I made sure and placed them near the correlating gas lines that ran throughout the wall next to the data housings." Radical justified his actions.

Circue laughed, "Yeah, not only did his own file get destroyed, but they lost a few more...hundred or so."

"The important thing is that nobody got hurt." Radical assured

"Miraculously." Motherboard responded. " And we won't be seeing their humanoid drones after us anymore."

"The glass is half full, in other words." Circue agreed with the other two.

Reaper stood not sure how to respond and shook his head. They were great at compromising for a lack of a better word. And he tried to ease his mind and believe that they had a good reason for their dire tactics. After nearly a year of multiple attempts to hack the CIA database and infiltrate their Research and Development departments, the group of three finally finished cleaning Radical's and Motherboard's records. Like before, they were now dead to the world beyond the Shadows of the Sun. Reaper was tired, and it was only going to help if he moved things forward, "It's time to get back on Provost and finally find him."

Radical noticed the dark rings under Reaper's eyes. "You look like death? Been sleeping much lately?"

Reaper turned and looked at him sharply, offended by his comment. "I'm not death. And no. No time to sleep till this is over."

Circuitcrusher giggled, "We better get started then. I cannot lose my heat streak right now. With all of these accomplishments racking up…"

Motherboard interrupted him, "I believe it's 'hot streak'."

"Whatever," Circue snapped, "Never-the-less, it's time to strike while the steel is hot."

Radical looked at him funny, "You don't get out much do you?"

"Alright," Reaper brought them back to attention, "I need you two to look at the data we recovered. Then we'll interrogate him once he wakes up while you cross check.

"You're very trusting to have him around." Motherboard looked at him through her glasses. The light reflected off of the glass which made her eyes barely visible. Her now longer brown hair dropped past her shoulders. "After all, he did work with our new target."

Reaper knew she had a point, "So did we, and I'm trying a new approach with him, the friendly one."

Circue laughed, "Why don't we buy him some toys to play with? Or I got it, how about a nice dinner and a movie?"

Reaper looked at him with a forced smile, "I guess you are coming along on the next assignment to catch Provost."

Circue's bright blue eyes widened and his mouth stayed closed.

"Now let's get to work," Reaper urged them. With that the group dispersed and he could hear Circue sniveling as they walked away. Reaper looked to see Boss looking stoic in silence. He approached the old Lazer Blade veteran. "Boss, you can chime in at any time in case I'm missing something."

Boss had no cigarette at this time, an unfamiliar sight, "You're doing well. Amongst the lack of sleep and the given the last 12 hours, you're doing better than I would."

"Can't say it's easy." Reaper scratched his head, "But this is just the beginning. We'll need to get all the intel we can in order to get the jump on Provost." He observed Boss carefully. The man had seen his team killed and hunted down, only to turn against each other and eventually fall. "What about you? Provost was your friend too."

"It doesn't matter what I think right now. Provost chose his path. And everyone must atone for their own decisions." Boss replied. "Your focus should be the objective at hand."

"Of course," Reaper acknowledged. He could see something was in Boss' eyes, perhaps it was resentment, but he had a good way of hiding it. If anyone could master feelings, it was Boss. How could he do it? After all, in the end he was still only human. But he was right, Reaper snapped, the mission came first. "I think Romeo may have hit him harder than I thought. We needed him out for the trip. Playing it safe, right?" Reaper nodded, "We will screen him when he wakes up."

Boss noticed his eyes, "You and the others should rest for a bit first."

Reaper nodded, unopposed to the orders, "Sure thing."

"You should be fresh for the interrogation. Remember, slow and easy questions, get to know him if you want to build his trust towards you." Boss's hoarse voice warned.

"Got it." Reaper walked towards the hallway. It was time to wait for the doctor to awaken from his coma.

Reaper lay awake yet again. Sleep was becoming more difficult to obtain. Especially when his mind flooded with images of the Academy. The team needed their rest, as well as the doctor. He needed to regain his consciousness after being knocked out.

Oracle made her way into his thoughts as well. To divert from her, he thought of Provost. What was he up to? Then he thought of Monster who was put on guard duty watching the doctor. They were getting closer to finding Provost than ever before. He would be surprised if any of the team was getting sleep right now. He figured the team needed some sleep due to the last 24 hours having been as rough as they were. He looked at the clock, 4:00 am. Yet another night when sleep would elude him.

The thought of his teacher was eating at him. Time was being wasted on rest. Then his mind flashed to Crosshair. The man was looking for his past; his father was alive and held the answers to his childhood. Reaper thought about his own, no parents and staying in a foster program all of his life. He thought about the others, the non-Shadows of the Sun. They all had lives before. He remembered Gothica had a fiancé. Amraam had parents, but unsure of any family since he never talked about them. Radical had remained single but still had family that raised him. Motherboard had claimed to be shunned by her family, but at least had one. Reaper found himself blacking out. It felt like a minute went by and his eyes shot open. The clock read 7:00 am. Finally, at least a few hours of sleep. The day was new and just getting started.

Reaper moved down the hallway hastily. After getting ready and into his usual attire, it was time to start playing the question game and gain enough information to finally pinpoint Provost's location and put an end to his scheme. At the cost of three lives and possibly more, Reaper was focused and determined to better his teacher. Since Provost was playing with them, it was time to change tactics and tread more carefully around suspected locations. How could he have been so close to them without them knowing? Reaper rubbed the back of his neck. The body scan results had come back normal. He did a mental assessment of his body to try and detect any changes. After checking the rest of his body in the showers for any other marks, it was safe to say that the P on his neck was the only close call. He thought about Oracle's comment, about the name. It did not make sense and now was not the time to analyze her riddles. Reaper was too focused on the task at hand, finding out where Provost Philp Johnson would be hiding next.

The room where the doctor stayed was large and a small bed sat in the corner. More like a prison cell, but it was the only secure enough place to put a questionable prisoner. Going against Gothica's advice, Reaper was sure of his judgement. The doctor would provide them with more leads than the half deleted data they collected anyway. He just needed to play it smart, and the doctor would open up and give him the information he wanted. Reaper nodded to Monster who stood along with Gothica to help ease the doctor into cooperating. Romeo was forbidden to join since his emotions were unstable. Normally, Reaper allowed Violet to help in questioning, but since she was distraught about Romeo and Julia, he figured she needed time to accept and move on.

Reaper gave Monster a nod and the large man pounded at the door, waking the doctor from his sleep. The doctor shot up from his bed.

"Wakey, wakey." Monster said.

"Dr. Hampton," Reaper approached the slide to view inside the room. "Good morning. You're safe from Philip. You're here with us." he tried to comfort the nervous man.

"Th, thank you?" Dr. Hampton anxiously answered. "Where am I?"

"Like he said, safe," Gothica chimed in. Her straight hair curled along her ears and stopped at her neck. It brought out her facial features and seemed to be easier to maintain. She continued, "Are you feeling okay?"

"Um," the doctor hesitated, "I suppose. Was knocking me out really necessary?"

"Yes," Reaper said, "More for our own protection since we seem to have some middle ground to build."

"Look, I got you the data and I've answered your questions. What do you want from me?" the doctor seemed stressed.

"Don't worry." Reaper continued, "Just a few more questions now that we can check the data and we'll let you go. You have my word."

"I've told you everything."

Monster approached the door. His sheer mass filled the peeping window to the room. "Am I gonna have to start breaking bones?"

"Monster, please. Not now." Gothica shook her head. "He's not going to." She assured the doctor.

The doctor took a deep breath. "Okay, fine. So from what I know, the three volunteers were tested and reacted very negatively towards the Enhancer Solution. One was killed by it. The remains and files regarding them were destroyed. Philip is one careful man." the doctor paced around his cell, reluctant to share more information.

"We know that." Reaper moved to the door, "What about Philip? What are his plans with the bodies of the other two?"

The doctor hesitated. "Philip was too careful. The data collected on them was kept tight and small. They were known as Project Phantom and Project Pandora. If the project had succeeded, Philip would have the data he needed to build a unit of super soldiers. As far as I know, they were comatose when he took them out of the lab. Neither had any brain activity. The Enhancer Solution was eating them from the inside. Some kind of chemical reaction to their bodies. It seemed as if they rejected it."

"Was Provost there?" Reaper looked at the ground, waiting for an answer.

The doctor was quiet, then confessed, "He had been there a few hours before you showed up. Yes. But he took them to another laboratory to run more tests." The doctor's voice was unsteady.

Gothica asked, "Did he use the solution on himself?"

The doctor looked up at her in surprise, "I, uh, I don't know. He mentioned something about able bodies. Did you all ever work with him?"

"Yeah, you could say that." Reaper proceeded with more questions, "Is there any information on the lab he moved them to?"

The doctor shook his head. "I really don't know. He never tells us. I just run the labs at that location he called, Ground Zero."

Reaper checked his comms to make sure they were transmitting, "Are you crosschecking his intel?"

Motherboard's voice announced over comms, "We've crosschecked the data. It's really just a small file about what he's telling you. No data on the dead volunteer. The only thing different is that Project Phantom and Project Pandora were two volunteers reported dead when he took them."

Reaper looked over at Gothica, "Damn. He's killed three people." He directed his attention to the comms. "Anything on his next stop?"

Motherboard continued, "At the end of the report here, it states something called Expo. And that's it."

Gothica thought, "Expo? Like some kind of Exposition? Maybe he's going to recruit more volunteers?"

Reaper met eyes with her, she could be right. "That's a pretty good possibility." He looked at the doctor, taking a seat on the corner of the bed. "Dr. Hampton, can you tell me anything on what Expo means?"

Dr. Hampton recollected, "Uh, I think I recall Philip saying something about it."

"What, when, and where?" Monster's deep voice resonated through the room.

"Uh, let me think. Philip said something about new clients. A meeting of some kind. Taking place this week." the doctor was concentrating.

"Did he say where?" Reaper spoke into comms, "Motherboard, check for any science or genetic expos throughout the US and other countries."

Monster looked over at Reaper, "It's Provost, remember? A little too blatant."

"Good point," Reaper thought about it, Provost would not be that easy. And if he was meeting for clients, a science expo would be too suspicious.

"Dr. Hampton, where?" Gothica urged him.

"I recall a place he said. The Big Apple. New York City." the doctor confessed.

"Motherboard, crosscheck." Reaper ordered.

"Checking now."

Reaper looked at Gothica, "New York, get the team ready for briefing." With that, she left. Monster stood tall and ready for his orders, "Monster, wanna catch an old friend?"

Monster smiled, "Finally. Something more than just petty mercenary or terrorist raids." he laughed.

Reaper awaited a response from Motherboard, "Getting antsy here."

"Patience." Motherboard responded, "Okay, I found something."

"Let's hear it."

"At eight o'clock this evening, at the Magnus Opera Convention Center. There is a Classical Art Expo tonight. And that's the only large Expo in New York this week."

"Art?" Monster raised his eyebrow. "Didn't think Provost had taste."

"Does an Art Expo ring a bell?" Reaper directed the question to the doctor.

"To be honest, Philip only mentioned an expo. I, I really don't know, I'm sorry, but I'm doing my best here." The doctor fidgeted around the room.

"Guess that's better than nothing. And if he's anything like his old colleagues, using massive crowds may be a better way to lose us if he knows we're there." Reaper thought hard about the clues. Coincidentally, they aligned with the intel. And according to his old teacher, there was no such thing as coincidences.

"Guess we can learn how to be art connoisseurs."
Monster chuckled.

"Reaper," Oracle's voice came through comms.

Reaper held up his hand to his ear. "What is it?"

She sounded spooked, "The ghost."

Reaper was impatient, "Oracle, please, not now."

She paused and he could hear her breath. "I'm afraid,
Boss is dead."

Chapter 10

The team converged on Boss's quarters. Reaper moved as fast as his legs would carry him. His mind raced through the images of what he would see. He found himself falling into thoughts of his old training regimen with Boss at his side. Teaching him the essentials of stealth, his primary weapon. His basics and advanced tactics in Grab Smash Kill. Boss was always full of wisdom. His one-liners of old sayings and experience is what he needed to hear sometimes to get back on track. In a strange way, Reaper already missed the smell of cigarettes. The possibility of his old mentor and teacher being dead made him hustle.

The team crowded around the room. Reaper made his way through the majority of them, only to find Gothica and Violet holding the motionless corpse. His face matched his gray hair. Blue eyes still open. Gothica looked up at Reaper and shook her head. The body was already cool to the touch. Violet had tears flowing down her face.

She struggled to speak, "I'm calling it....Time of death, maybe an hour ago."

"What happened? Heart attack?" Reaper tried to make sense of the situation.

Gothica shook her head, "Possibly, it looks as if he just collapsed right here on the floor."

Reaper looked down at the floor and saw that just a few feet away from Boss's dead fingers was a cold burnt out cigarette half smoked. The room was clean, just as Boss had kept it. No signs of anyone else in the room. It did not make sense. He turned to see Romeo making his way in. He froze at the sight of the old man on the floor. Romeo stood for a second then backed out slowly. Reaper saw the others eager to enter. He held a finger up to signal them to wait. He needed to check the scene first. Then he thought of someone who may help, "Oracle, can you come in here, please?"

She was fitted into her custom sneaking suit. Looking ready and able, Reaper needed her to "look" around. "Oracle, how did you know? What happened here?"

Her marble eyes seemed to wander around the small room. She held her hands as if feeling the air around her. "Truth, will get us killed. The ghost from the Academy."

Reaper tried to allow her riddles, "Oracle, not now. There's no time. What happened?"

Oracle turned to look at him, "Did you see the name, it's misspelled."

"Who are you talking about?" Reaper raised his voice.

"Provost's shadows." Oracle started to move around the room. "Boss's neck will show the cause of death."

Reaper was lost, she was indirect as much as she was too direct with her advice. It was beginning to frustrate him. "Gothica? What do you see?" He was feeling desperate. He noticed Violet struggling. "Violet, please, I know this is hard, but focus."

Violet lifted her head and gripped tightly onto her braided hair. Her eyes were filled with tears, then she looked back down at the body and moved the head to get a better look at the neck area. The letter P was carved into his skin. Then a faint wavy red line seemed to flow across the higher part of his neck.

Oracle broke the silence, "The P from the letter."

Reaper wanted to yell, but it made sense. The P on their necks was written the exact way it was signed on Provost's letter. "Oracle, he was here?"

She looked at him, "It is, hard to see."

"Keep looking then," Reaper ordered. "Violet, what's that on his neck?"

Violet struggled to keep her eyes clear. She looked up at Oracle and shook. Gothica took her hand. "It's okay." Gothica tried assuring her.

Violet slightly nodded, "It looks like a bruise, as if force was applied here pre-death." She struggled to speak, "As if he was choked."

Reaper closed his eyes in frustration, "Provost killed his own friend." He opened his eyes to see if Oracle would be of any help, but she stood still like she was afraid of something.

Gothica stood up, "That means he could be close. He couldn't have gotten far within the last hour."

Reaper thought for a second. He looked up as if to find the answer but instead noticed a symbol. The *P vs R* that they had seen back on the Academy walls were now on the ceiling of Boss's room at the Nest! "I never thought Philip played games like this."

"It's sick," Gothica spoke up and addressed the others, "Search the Nest, check the doctor, he could be next."

"Monster's still with him." Reaper mumbled. "I don't believe this." He found himself falling into doubt, again. Something he had not felt since his failed attempts at chasing their last great foe, James Camelot. "Provost baited us. He used the doctor to distract us. Knowing we'd be too caught up with him and searching for him too. He used that to slip right in, without us knowing. He killed Boss right under our noses."

Gothica looked around, "I guess that it is safe to say, he's alive."

Reaper analyzed his next foe, Philip Johnson, the man that trained them. The same man that molded them into the warriors they had become. As far as the team's limits could go, he pushed them further. But had he given up all of his secrets? Had Provost hid key tactics from them? How was he going to be beaten?

Oracle's voice distracted him, "You ask too many questions. But not the right ones."

Reaper looked up at her, he could see her trying to help, but it was time to move, not think. "We're going to that convention." He addressed everyone over comms, "Secure the Nest. Meet back in briefing in half an hour."

The briefing room was quiet. And the smell of cigarette smoke would no longer fill room. As if Boss's essence was gone. It was sobering and going to take time to get used to. Reaper tried to collect his thoughts. For Provost to be so close to them and killing one of them was a terrifying realization. The Nest had been infiltrated by its creator. Right from beneath them, he had snuck in to kill Boss. And that made the Nest just as hostile as any warzone. As far as he knew, the Nest was unsafe and unfit as the headquarters for now.

"We need to get important things out and lock this place down, and not come back until this is over." Reaper said. "We are going to abandon the Nest. Once we've secured and terminated the threat of Provost and his clients, then, and only then will it be safe." The team stood idle.

Then Gothica broke the silence. "What about all the medical facilities here?"

Reaper thought of them, the Nest was equipped with state of the art medical equipment. From production labs of the Adrenaline Solution to the massive healing tanks where wounded teammates could undergo surgeries and heal within the complex liquid solution.

"It's a sacrifice we have to make for now." Reaper stated. He looked around the room, "Oracle, Monster, Circue, Gothica, and myself will attend the Expo."

"Aw," Circue tried to keep it quiet but the others heard and looked over at him. He gritted his teeth with a nervous smile, "Sorry."

Reaper looked at Monster who held the doctor in restraints, "The doc can stay with the team here. Provost could be after him next."

"Hey, hey," The doctor rejected nervously, "No offense, but Philip came in and killed your CO. Who is to say he's not coming to get me from here? Besides, look." The doctor pulled down his collar to show the letter P on his neck. "I'm marked too. Logically, it would be easier if I were there. In a public place, if Philip finds me, it may be easier for you to find him."

Reaper observed the nervous doctor, "How did he get to you?"

"Back at Ground Zero perhaps? Look," the man looked around at the team, suffering a barrage of glaring eyes, "I mean, Philip may still need the data. He gave me that responsibility and told me to give it to him as soon as I could. I knew about the expo and if I am there I can coax him out of hiding."

"Eager to go?" Gothica asked.

"I'm not exactly safe anywhere, apparently. But at least let me try to get his attention to expose him and give him to you, so to speak." The doctor appeared sincere.

Reaper looked over at Oracle, "What do you think?"

Oracle stood still, as if looking through the doctor, "The ghost will be there."

"Fine," Reaper cut, "Bring him. I'll stay with him while we're there. The rest of you will spread out and search for our target."

The doctor nodded, "Uh, thank you." he wiped the sweat from his forehead with his shoulder.

Gothica looked over at Reaper and whispered, "Monster and Circue are coming with us, really?"

Taking into account Gothica's advice, Romeo needed to be away from the mission area. Using him to look for Provost at the Nest would make better use of him. If Provost was close, or if he had help, the team here could manage. Reaper thought about his approach, "Circue needs to be there. Set up a perimeter with your scanners. Monster, of course, if anything big happens. Romeo is patrolling the outer Nest perimeter. He's better off here with the rest. Violet needs time to grieve. She could be a liability out there. Motherboard," He looked at her. "Close the Nest down. Amraam can take Radical to finish sweeping the area for threats and move the team out of here. After the area is clear, take the team to the safe house at these designated coordinates." The coordinates revealed a small valley complex on the hologram screen. It was in the mountains a few hundred miles away.

"He's taking us, Crush!" Monster laughed and slugged him in the arm.

"Ow," Circue grabbed his arm. "I connected the dots, thanks."

Reaper felt rushed, but the mission, and Provost came first. He did his best to balance the team from mentally unstable with those who were still fit. "The Ark will drop us off, comeback here and take you to the designated safe house location. It's time to stay low and off the grid so Provost can't track us. We'll get him at the expo. And he'll pay." He observed the four of them. "Okay, let's go get him."

Section 2:

The Opera

Chapter 11

The large art expo filled the Magnus Opera Convention Center. Frames filled with classical art littered the large wall that faced the entrance. Along the other walls were more pieces of contemporary art by established and unknown artists. It was a good place to meet new artists and become famous. It was also the next place to find a cold blooded murderer. Perfect lighting allowed for the pictures to be seen in optimal condition. People filled every corner of the vast room and only broken up by a few music kiosks and a bar that served adult beverages. Classical music filled the ceiling of the room. A large prompter displayed the song handwritten by whoever had requested it.

Now it was time to pretend to be a part of society once again. Reaper looked over at Oracle who was wearing a smooth pearl colored dress. Her hair was immaculate. Glowing in a room fit for lighting art. As much as Reaper tried to focus on the mission, seeing her in formal attire was making him wander again. She was forced to wear a pair of sophisticated glasses that hid her eyes. That way no one would get too suspicious that a blind woman was looking at art. Gothica stood next to Oracle, holding her hand and guiding her inconspicuously through the crowded room. She wore a familiar dress. A blue dress that fell to her knees but still allowed her to hide her crossbow pistol. Her newly styled hair seemed to fit her face perfectly. Both Monster and Circue looked surprisingly comfortable in normal attire, though very out of place at this event, their cover was security guards. Reaper hoped that their clumsy play would cease in this public place. Not to mention he needed to split up Circue from Radical and Motherboard so they would not try to blow up or burn any of the art. Reaper stayed close to the doctor who looked more comfortable in public than the team. His dirty blond hair fell past his ears, parted to the left. His glasses were still fixed on his face. Each of them wore a name tag attached to their outfits on the left side of the chest. All but Dr. Hampton used aliases, other than Gothica who stuck to her old name, A. Marshall.

Reaper looked over at Circue, whose name tag read a bizarre alias, Chuck Jaeger. "I think people will be slightly disappointed that you aren't the real thing."

Circue smiled, "They don't have to know, and judging by this crowd, I sincerely doubt they even know who he is."

Monster laughed, "Too busy looking at paint and not like ol' Crush here," He motioned to Circue, "who's always looking through his collection of air plane stickers."

"Hey," Circue tried to defend but Monster interrupted.

"Maybe there are some planes painted here, let's go see." He grabbed Circue and hauled him off.

"Maybe they'll have pictures of teepees here." Circue snickered back. "To remind you of home or something."

Reaper watched the two wander into the crowd. Maybe it was not a good idea to have them in the crowd of art enthusiasts. "Uh, you two get back here. Provost could spot you from the other side of the city. Start looking around the surrounding rooms throughout this building. At least try to blend in as security guards."

"Maybe this is why we haven't taken these two out on missions like this." Gothica butted in. "I mean a satellite could pinpoint those two in here from space."

Reaper shook his head. He knew better, but he needed them away from the Nest and instead somewhere in which Provost could be showing up at any time. Hopefully the security guard angle would help keep them busy and out of trouble. Had some of the others not been in rough shape mentally, and Monster and Circue having had emotional ties with Boss, then the selection of infield operatives would have been different. Putting his trust in Romeo was out of the question. He would certainly kill Provost if given the chance. Now was not the time for Radical's spontaneous antics and since he had no ties, his clear head could help the others. Motherboard needed to secure the Nest networks before they left to the safe house. Amraam needed to stay to help keep Violet on track. Though relationships and feelings were prohibited, Reaper knew they were an inevitable human trait. And he could not judge since he found himself falling for his newest recruit, Oracle. The entire team ran through his mind. Would they manage?

"Oracle, you see anything?" Reaper asked her, waiting for some kind of vision from her showing where Provost could be hiding.

She turned to look and examine the doctor, then his name tag, "They misspelled his name."

The doctor looked down at his name tag, it read How Hampton. "No, they just couldn't fit my full name."

Reaper looked at Oracle, "Anything on Provost?"

She looked around, as if observing the crowd, "The ghosts are hiding."

"What does that mean?" Reaper asked.

Oracle looked at each of them, then looked at Reaper, as if she was scared of something, but kept silent.

Reaper shook his head. Her riddles were hard to grasp, but he knew she only spoke that way. "Let's spread out and look for him."

They dispersed. Oracle had little trouble navigating the dense crowd. Gothica broke away from her and headed more in Reaper's direction with the doctor a few feet in front. She reached Reaper, "We should try to blend in a little bit. I think Oracle will fit in with this crowd just fine."

Reaper caught the sarcasm in her words, "Yeah, this crowd looks terrifying." He observed groups of people, the ones in what would be deemed modern and stylish attire. Then the ones dressed in bright colored clothes. A diverse crowd full of peculiarity.

Gothica observed Reaper, he seemed to have something on his mind. "Something you want to talk about?"

Reaper bowed his head. The realization that Boss had been killed from under their noses had not set in yet. A strange feeling that he would go back to the Nest and smell Boss's cigarette again felt real. But it would never happen. Guilt set in, that the rest of the team was struggling, while Crosshair got a vacation out of it. "I guess I still don't believe that Boss is dead. How could I?"

Gothica tried comforting him, "Because, you know our mission and the man we're after is very capable."

"True." Reaper thought hard about the circumstances, her intuition was spot on. "I guess I just didn't see Provost for as ruthless as he is."

"Given his past and the fact he ordered us to take out his old team? As for Boss…well, things were personal." Gothica thought back to her CIA espionage days. "Sometimes those who are close, tend to be the worst enemies."

"The team doesn't deserve this. Any of it." Reaper said as the two approached the bar just few feet away from the doctor, who was looking at a painting. "And I shouldn't have allowed Crosshair to leave. Not at this time."

"Sometimes reuniting with the past is what helps us in our future. Home is where he needs to be right now." Gothica justified their decision to allow Crosshair's leave.

Reaper looked at her, the smooth classical music made him feel less tense. He noticed her name tag. A. Marshall. "What about you?" He signaled to her name tag. "Why that name, again?" He was curious as to why she chose to use her real name again.

Gothica looked down at her name tag. "Couldn't make one up I liked. Besides, it's who I used to be."

Reaper looked down in shame for a second. Thoughts about her life before them flashed at what could have been. "Missing it?"

"Of course," Gothica smiled, "Wouldn't you?"

"Maybe." Reaper looked at her. "What would you have done? You know, if Gothica didn't exist."

Gothica raised her brow at him. "I don't think about that much. Maybe married, maybe not."

Reaper tried to sound heartfelt, "Did your fiancé and you end things on a bad note?"

"No actually," Gothica smiled, "he and I agreed that once I realized my career was not more important than him, he would have me back. Of course, that's been a couple years."

"That's good at least." Reaper grinned at her, "Don't need to burn the bridges due to priorities. You're goal oriented, if he didn't respect that, then I guess that makes things easier to accept."

"Wow," Gothica tapped his arm, "You're full of good advice today."

"Don't get used it." Reaper laughed, "Any family?"

"Yes, actually my mom." Gothica seemed unfazed by the questions. As if it were easy to just go back and forth, from mission and grief, to family and happiness. Something Reaper could not master.

He could only feel pity for recruiting her. "Did you have a good relationship?"

Gothica's tone shifted, she was quiet, "Well, off and on."

"Had a hard time accepting your career choice?"

"Yeah," Gothica looked up and around the room, "Guess you could say that. Mom took my decisions pretty hard. Didn't like me in danger."

"Sorry." Reaper felt guilt slip in.

Gothica looked at him and squinted her eyes, "Why?"

He struggled with what he would say next. He recalled Boss' ability to hide his feelings and pain. It was something that Reaper was beginning to fail at. "Sometimes I feel like I killed whatever life you may have had."

"Well for starters, I made that decision to join you guys. I made the decision with my career in the CIA." Gothica argued, "And I make my own decisions in life. It's served me well," She slowed down, realizing what she was saying, "at the cost of my loved ones."

He nodded, "If it means anything now, I hope one day you get to reconcile with them. And I really hope Crosshair finds closure as well. I think sometimes, we all need it."

She shook her head at him, "Provost really has you thinking, huh?"

Reaper bit his lip, "He's like a father. Boss was like a father. That makes this more difficult."

She could tell he struggled with the subject, "Think about it this way. He's your mission, even if it's just to find him. Focus on that. You're pretty good at obsessing about your target, apply a fraction of that here, and I think you'll be fine."

He looked up and grinned, "You're right, we need to locate Provost before he locates us. Spread out and keep your eyes open."

"That's the spirit." She winked.

He acknowledged Gothica's mentor-like advice, "Thanks." They parted ways and he worked his way into the crowd and close to the doctor. He appeared to be requesting a song on the juke box. He finished writing and slipped the piece of paper into the machine.

The doctor looked up and was startled by Reaper approaching him closely. "Oh, sorry. I thought I would make a request, one of my favorites." He slipped the paper inside the machine. "Any luck?"

Reaper could tell the doctor was nervous, "Not yet, just stay calm and low." He adjusted his long sleeve shirt to fluff out the wrinkles on his arm. Then looked back at the doctor, feeling that Oracle's senses may hold something. But he could not think of what. None of the riddles were making sense.

"I'm doing my best." Dr. Hampton said. "Enjoying the art at least?"

He looked at the paintings around him, "I guess you could say that." The two moved further down the wall.

The doctor turned around and smiled, "I have been eyeing a nice piece that's walking around here." He looked around to try and spot the person he was referring to. Then he saw a woman in the crowd, "Her."

Reaper followed his eyes and spotted the woman standing a little ways away from them. She was tall, over six feet with high heels. Her green eyes complemented her olive skin. Her long dark hair dropped evenly to her back and styled in a wavy fashion. Her dress was mixed from light brown to dark. He noticed her long legs. Her calves were tight and fit. He followed the dress to her torso. The straps hung over her strong shoulders. She looked over at them and away. Then walked on, disappearing into the crowd. "That is a pleasant sight."

Dr. Hampton laughed, "See I think I have good taste. So you guys get out much, uh, Reaper right? Any family?"

"No, just teammates." he responded observing the crowd.

"Ah, well, I guess you all stay pretty busy to have any time for them." the doctor gazed at the art on the wall. "I can't imagine that the state your mind is in." The doctor said. "I mean, these last two days seem to have been quite tolling on you guys."

"Yeah, you could say that."

"I mean, really, you have my admiration. I know Philip was an intense individual. And you guys seem to have a pretty deep relationship with him."

"You're very perceptive, Doc." Reaper grinned.

"My job." Dr. Hampton said, "I have to be. But I am serious. I really do admire your courage. Can't wait to see you all in action."

Reaper was flattered, but he felt that the gratitude was unnecessary, "Hopefully, you don't have to."

"Ah, this is my favorite painting so far." the doctor stopped and removed his glasses to admire the painted canvas.

Reaper turned and immediately fell into a trance. The picture was of an aurora borealis over a decimated city. The contrast of beauty and destruction was obviously the painter's goal. He felt himself remember his dreams, when Aurora spoke to him. He mumbled to the doctor, "You do have good taste." The painting triggered emotion in him. He felt himself longing for Aurora's voice to speak to him. But instead the moment was interrupted by the doctor speaking more.

"You know, uh, Reaper, I think your team is tough, but are you really sure we should be looking for Philip with all of you in a depressed state of mind?"

He mumbled back to the doctor, "We'll be fine. Both you and us have some business to discuss with our ex-colleague."

"It worries me though. You know, the uncertain hero is often more dangerous than the relentless villain." the doctor said.

Reaper heard the words. They sounded familiar. His trance was loosening as the words were breaking it up.

"You know, this painting is the type that if you look closely, you find something hidden within." the doctor spoke again. But Reaper was too deep in thought. Those words had come from Provost's letter. The doctor commented, "Ah, finally my song request."

He gazed at the painting again, deeper in thought; then an image started to appear. P vs R. The same symbol. Reaper broke his trance, with a deep breath he looked back at the doctor taking off his glasses. A new song began to play. It was a familiar tune. He recalled it being the song about the phantom that haunted the opera house. On the prompter, the written request displayed for all to see. Reaper noticed the handwriting. It matched the letter from Provost. The word phantom written out with the same signature style as Provost's signature. Reaper's heart rate sped up. His breathing becoming shallow. He looked back at the doctor, who smiled with confidence on his face. Reaper looked down at his name tag, How Hampton. Reaper thought about Oracle's words, and his name being misspelled. He looked up at the prompter then back at the name tag. The letters were the same. Hampton......Phantom!

Chapter 12

Reaper stepped back slowly in shock, "You're…."

The man who stood in front of him smiled and shook his head. His demeanor had changed. He was no longer the scared doctor. "Reaps, that took you way longer than I expected."

Reaper felt weak in the knees. "Phantom? You're not dead?"

"You really do put clues together slowly." Phantom laughed, "I expected, after all the hype that Philip fed me, for you to be better, honestly."

He felt nauseous, thinking of Provost's suicide letter. "The letter?"

"Yes," Phantom nodded, "A tactic used to keep you busy while we prepared. I'll give you that one, since it would be next week by the time you figured out who wrote it."

His breathing increased, his vision becoming blurry. "But...how? The mark?" he referred to the mark of the letter P on his neck.

"Mark of death, I'm afraid." Phantom smiled wide.

Reaper took another slow step back, his nose caught a soothing scent of perfume. He turned to his right and was frightened by a woman's face nearly on his shoulder. THE woman. The one the doctor, or rather Phantom had pointed out earlier. Her beautiful complexion and piercing green eyes seemed to cut through him.

"Allow me to introduce you, Reaps. This is Pandora." Phantom held his hand out. "Death, personified." he called her.

Reaper tried to react, he moved his hand with quick reflexes to try and strike Phantom, but his arm was held back. It was strange, Pandora was holding it and he could not budge her grip. He turned his wrist to shake loose and attempt a throw, but she broke his stance and held him back. He struggled, but careful not to make a scene, "Where's number three?"

"Oh, he is dead. Body couldn't handle it." Phantom said, "Pandora, please, it's okay, go entertain the others while we have a chat."

Reaper was released and turned to face her but she was gone, as she had disappeared into the crowd. He turned his attention to Phantom. His chest felt heavy with guilt and shame for not figuring it out. Oracle tried to tell him, the ghost, the name, but he did not want to listen. Was she and Gothica next? He needed to warn them. He reached for his ear to initiate his comms.

"Don't worry," Phantom said, "I have a transmitter blocking all of your transmissions. This needs to just stay between us."

"You killed Boss." Reaper said quietly, careful not to start a panic.

"Perhaps." Phantom tilted his head to the side. "The ventilation in that place is quite good. When you're like me, small places are as easy to navigate as an open field. Monster grew too predictable with his check patterns."

"Drinks, gentlemen?" a waiter holding a tray of small drinks with glass stirring rods approached the two.

"Yes," Reaper grabbed a drink and held it.

"No, thank you." Phantom smiled and waited for the server to leave then continued. "It was easy to act as a scientist, especially with how tenacious you guys are. I will admit that Philip talked highly of you when working on us. But he wanted us to be better."

"Where is he?" Reaper held the drink in his hand securely; he pulled the stirring rod out and held it in his other hand, ready to fight in a second's notice.

"Oh, alive and well. Somewhere in this city."

Reaper felt little relief.

Phantom moved closer to him. "Let me tell you a little about myself. Now, I like challenges. Once he told us about the Cleansing Blade and his hopes to improve upon them, I was intrigued. Volunteered and became even more. So, I made a plan. To see the Cleansing Blade in action; impressive? Maybe a little. But you changed the name and seem to be slower than I was told I would see. Though, Oracle seems to be the only smart one of the bunch."

Reaper gritted his teeth in shame. Oracle was right all along. Though she spoke in strange riddles and phrases, she was still right. "So then what do you want?"

"I thought, I have to see this Cleansing Blade. So, Pandora and I decided it was time to meet you. I will admit I was thrown off by you being at the Academy so soon. But I improvised and devised a new plan. To test you further."

"So what's with the symbols?"

"Oh, you mean the P vs R? That would be me, and you, dear Reapmeister." Phantom kept a sinister smile across his face. "I mean, what better battle, than the Grim Reaper himself, hunted down by the Dark Phantom."

"You think this is a sick game?" Reaper prepared himself to take a shot with his stirring rod and try to finish Phantom now.

"Yes," Phantom observed him, "that's exactly what this is."

Reaper stepped towards him and quietly shoved the rod at Phantom. He felt his hand stop. Phantom yanked the rod from his hand and shoved it up into Reaper's sleeve.

"Better put that away before these art heads start getting excited."

Reaper did not listen, he sidestepped showing his back to the crowd while he attempted another take down. He grabbed his glass and two made quick strikes towards each other. But Phantom quickly grabbed his other hand and twisted his wrist, forcing Reaper's fingers to loosen the grip on his glass. Allowing it to smash against the floor.

"Ah, clumsy, Reaps." Phantom played it off as an accident, a server approaching with towels. "We're sorry; some of us don't know our place when it comes to standing too close."

Reaper looked up, the thought of a panicking crowd made him cautious of his next move. The broken glass could be a weapon, but the cost of innocent people getting hurt was not worth it. He would have to allow Phantom to have his fun.

"Come on, let's keep moving." Phantom signaled for Reaper to follow. Reluctantly, Reaper stood up and proceeded down the long wall of art, staying close to Phantom. "Now, do you really want to make things difficult for yourself? I mean, a room filled with innocent people and such," Phantom held his hands out, "beautiful art."

Reaper looked around, trying to spot Oracle and Gothica. They were nowhere in sight. If Phantom and Pandora were improvements upon what Provost had started with the Cleansing Blade, what kind of surprises did they possess? "So, you guys are a product of genetic enhancements?"

"Intrigued, Reaps?" the two walked slowly down the wall of art. "Yes. Provost wanted to see how genes of warriors, like yourselves and ours, could be changed, improved, to be made better. The Enhancer Solution took well for us two. The genetic codes combined and allowed for rapid adaptation. In turn, we became better than the Cleansing Blade, or whatever you may call yourselves now."

"So, Provost wanted more," Reaper felt disappointed in his old teacher. "What's he planning with you then?"

"Planning on sitting back, and enjoying the show." Phantom kept his sinister smile. "I wouldn't put too much thought into him at the moment, because you have your plate full right now."

"So, what is it that you want?"

"Our mission is simple." Phantom faced him, "To destroy the Cleansing Blade."

The words echoed in his chest. Reaper wrapped his head around the circumstances. "So let me get this straight, Provost needed a team to eliminate his own. And now, he needs another team to eliminate what he's created?"

"A vicious cycle huh, Reaps?"

"So, you started with Boss?" Reaper kept his voice down. "And now you're going to work your way down?"

"What does it feel like, Reaps?" Phantom kept smiling, "To know that you're targeted? To know that you are inferior?"

Reaper grew tired of hearing him talk, "Then let's leave this party. And you can accomplish your mission without anybody else getting hurt. Or are you afraid?"

Phantom's smile grew from ear to ear. "I've been longing. Enough hiding in a crowd. Let's see if we can find out if your team has met with Pandora yet."

Reaper quickly let out a short breath. Was Pandora going to kill them? Was she capable of such a task? He needed to find his team. He looked through the crowd as he followed Phantom through the dense group of art enthusiasts. But Oracle and Gothica were out of sight. Horrible thoughts entered his mind. Were they dead? He tried to remember Gothica's words, advice that even Aurora had given him. To keep his faith in his team. Reaper felt little comfort in the thought, but it was all he had. And right now, it was time to put Phantom's threat to an end.

Chapter 13

Monster and Circuitcrusher patrolled a smaller art room. Filled with statues, ranging from the infamous David and Goliath, to the replication of Mona Lisa in stone form. No Provost around. And the dense crowds of people made it hard to locate anybody suspicious. But the six foot six inch Monster had no trouble making his way through the tight groups. Circue stayed close behind, fiddling with his flex screen pad he managed to strap onto his social attire. He stared at Monster in semi-formal attire. It was strange to the see the giant killer without his custom sneaking suit and large weapons. Even having his thick long hair down and fixed nicely made Circue jealous.

"Feeling naked without your handkerchief?" Circue asked. "Not used to seeing all your hair."

Monster looked at him and smiled, "Not used to a lot of hair in general, are you?" He teased, "Besides, you could use a hanky since I'm sure you feel pretty naked up there all the time."

"Hey!" Circue caught himself in public as people staring made him uncomfortable. He grinned awkwardly, and whispered to Monster. "You're just jealous you can't grow a moustache."

"You're right." Monster said sarcastically. "At least that's one reason to need a comb."

Circue squinted at him, "At least I need a razor."

"You could just shave your head." Monster laughed as Circue's face started to turn red. He went back to fiddling with his flex pad. Monster walked down to see a small statue, "Find anything you like?"

Circue was not paying attention, and smacked into Monster. Nearly knocking him off balance and into the fragile statue. "Oops."

Monster tried to keep his voice low. "I break it, you're buying it."

"Sorry," Circue could almost feel the stares at him in the art lobby, "All of this art is making me think…"

"So that's really what causes it?" Monster laughed.

"What? No!" Circue rubbed his scalp, "I mean I'm designing some new. Uh," He remembered he was surrounded by civilians, "Assistant devices."

"You should invent a device that allows you to see in front of you when you're walking. Now come on, let's look around the lobby some more." Monster walked towards the exit of the art statue room. He turned to check the lobby, then checked the other way. He spotted a woman walking alone wearing a dark brown dress and long, dark wavy hair. He started to admire the new scenery. She turned to look at him, her physic was alluring. Then she smiled at the two.

Circue began to sweat profusely, "Did you see that? She looked at me."

Monster turned to him, "You might be right, you're melting."

"No, I'm serious. Wow, she is the only art here worth looking at." Circue stumbled over his words.

"Calm down, Crush." Monster looked back to spot the woman walking further down the hallway approaching the large exposition room. He looked back at Circue pouring with sweat. "You're gonna need a life jacket."

"She looks pretty suspicious if you ask me. We should tail her." His bright blue eyes watched her turn into the main expo. She turned around and gave him another alluring glance.

"Easy," Monster watched her walk. "Let's approach her slowly. She obviously wants us to follow." Her green eyes seemed to magnetize them. The two stood up straight and proceeded to tail her into the large art expo. Thanks to his grand size and height, Monster could see above most of the art nerds and spotted the woman walking towards the back of the room.

As they both navigated through the dense crowd, Monster's eye caught sight of Gothica hastily approaching them.

"Are you guys' deaf?" Gothica scolded them, "Can't you hear me on the comms?" She kept her voice down.

"No," Circue defended, "Why would we ignore your calls?"

She ignored the sarcasm this time, "I saw Reaper leave with the doctor. And since you guys are out I thought you'd met up with them. He's usually really good about keeping us posted. So that has me worried." Gothica looked up at Monster, "Have you seen them?"

"No," Monster's deep voice replied, "I haven't. And no signs of Provost, either."

Gothica looked around, "Maybe Reaper found something and took the doctor out. What are you doing?" She watched Circue playing on his flexible screened pad.

"Searching," Circue's eyes lit up, "Ah hah!" He yelled, causing people to stop talking and look at him. He began to sweat more. "Sorry." he kept his voice down, "I found something interesting. I think Reaper never contacted us for the same reason we couldn't hear you."

"And why's that?" Gothica asked.

"Our comms are down. It appears there is a signal blocking them." Circue studied his pad.

"If you find it, can you get rid of it?" Gothica looked around the crowd, searching for Oracle, who also seemed to be missing.

"Uh, well that's the interesting part." Circue looked at both of them, "It resembles our same frequency codes, like it's our own frequency blocking itself."

"I take that as a no then." Gothica shook her head. "We need to find him, and Oracle."

"Got it." Monster stood up, "Let's keep looking."

"I'll see if I can find Reaper and Dr. Hampton in the lobby." Gothica exited the expo.

Circue glanced over at Monster, "Provost could be using this signal. I think he spotted us first."

Monster looked around. "What are we waiting for? Let's see if we can find out where he's hiding." The large man finished his sentence as soon as he spotted the woman they were following earlier. Now, she looked right at him from a distance, opening a door in the back leaving the expo. He took it as probable cause to follow. "Let's check the staff only areas."

"Good idea," Circue said, "That's what I was gonna say."

Monster and Circuitcrusher moved through the crowd and approached the door. The two bumped into each other as they both tried walking through the doorway. "Excuse me." Monster snapped. The two emerged into a dark hallway with a maintenance closet a few yards down. The musty smell of cleaning equipment filled the hall. It seemed to continue down with ducts and pipes along the ceiling. But no sign of the woman.

Circue kept close. "Should have brought the Cat-Eyes."

"You mean that wrist pad doesn't come with a flashlight app?" Monster teased, "Come on, Crush, you're slacking."

"Guess I have a new project to work on." Circue said. "And it will have way more apps."

They walked down the hallway in sync with their steps. More doorways seemed to branch off in the distance as they approached a maintenance room. Monster stuck his head in, but no one was inside. The hallway's dim light made the narrow passage eerie. Circue stepped forwards, wiping his forehead and drenching his sleeve with sweat. He felt a hand grab onto his shoulder and let out a squeal that echoed down the hallway.

"Crush, take it easy." Monster laughed, "You're too tense. Now check that room over there." he pointed to the next doorway.

"Uh, are you sure?" Circue hesitated.

"What's the matter, afraid of the dark?" Monster asked, "There are no such things as monsters. Don't sweat it."

"Easy for you to say." Circue proceeded towards the door. He struggled to see down the dim hallway. Approaching the doorway slowly, his eyes caught a dark figure standing still in the hall. It did not move. "Uh, Slam?" he called to Monster.

"Yes,"

"What's that?" Circue turned to him and pointed down the hall.

"What's what?" Monster responded. "Can't see anything."

Circue looked back and saw nothing. "Whew. Man, is it hot in here? I think we passed by a drink stand in the expo, I'm just gonna go get something and be right back."

"No, you're not," Monster walked towards him, "Now go check your area."

"Yeah, okay fine." Circue swallowed and approached the door. His shaky hand grabbed the handle and turned the knob, it was locked. "Oh, thank God." He whispered to himself. Circue then backed away and turned to look down the hallway. The figure stood again. The low light made it difficult to make out what it was, but that only a human silhouette could be made out.

Circue held his breath, then the figure moved, as if hovering towards him. He let out a squeal that vibrated the pipes above him. Then the figure shot off to the left.

"Crush, jeez, would you keep it down?" Monster snapped, "What the hell is your problem?"

Circue shook out of his fear, "I, I, I thought I saw something hover towards me. This door is locked."

Monster looked down the hall to see nothing, "I think you're going crazy. Now check that room up there to the left, and I'll break that locked door."

"You sure?" Circue hesitated to step forward, "I can try this door again."

"Go Crush!"

"Okay, I'm going." Circue took baby steps towards the next doorway. Unsure of what he saw, he took a second to catch his breath. He checked down the hallway and was slightly put at ease with the sight of nothing there. Then he turned and approached the door that was cracked open. He took a deep breath and wiped his forehead again. The light of the wrist pad dimly lit the doorway. The door creaked as it swung open. He let out a breath in relief as he noticed some old table linens stored on the shelf. He looked closer to see what appeared as the figure, and it moved right for him. He flinched as the figure attacked him. Circue jumped back and found himself defending against the beautiful woman. Circue knew enough of Grab Smash Kill techniques to utilize them in the field. Despite having no desire to fight up close.

However, the woman was lightning fast. Circue found himself being turned around and his arm aching. She had ripped off his wrist pad and shoved him against the adjacent hall. Circue slammed against the wall but turned to see the woman. In her hands, his flex screen wrist pad. His heart sank as she crushed it. The pieces fell to the floor like crumbs. Circue gasped, "How could you?"

Monster caught the sound of Circue whining. He tilted his head back to see what was wrong. He noticed that he was not alone, but rather that the beautiful woman they were following was actually attacking Circue. Monster moved to aid his friend and met eyes with the woman. She turned back to Circue and grabbed his arm, yanking him towards her. Monster watched her turn him around and plant a side kick into his lower back. Forcing him against the wall with a thunderous impact. Circue's limp body crumbled to the floor.

Monster made an attempt to subdue the woman. He looked down at Circue on the floor, still breathing. He gazed at the woman and attacked without hesitation. His massive size made her seem insignificant, but that made no difference. She dodged his attack and grabbed his arm. Her hands moved towards his wrist and cranked it around, causing him to lose balance. Monster endured the pain and lifted her off the ground, slamming her into the vent duct above. She anticipated the attack and thrust her high heel shoe into his ribs. Monster held her up against the ceiling despite the pain shooting from his chest. The woman kicked again and landed her shoe in the same spot. He jolted slightly from the pain. She had enough time to grab his hand and torque his finger back far enough to break.

The woman came down with Monster's arm still in her grasp. The strength of Monster was unrelenting as he grabbed her with his other hand and threw her down the hallway. Her body twisted in the air. Like a cat, she landed on all fours. Her movement was fast, faster than Monster had ever seen before. She stood up to face him. He moved his hand around and grabbed his finger to reset it. With a quick snap, it was back in socket. His shirt felt wet from where she had kicked him. He touched his ribs to notice two felt slightly indented. He checked his fingers and saw blood. Monster kept his eyes on the woman and moved his head back and forth to prepare for another tussle. He was uncertain of who she was, or perhaps what. She moved abnormally fast, but her techniques were strangely familiar. She was strong, but she felt human. The only sure thing was he planned on making her pay for what she did to his teammate.

Monster let out an earth shattering roar as he watched the woman move so fast and with such precision, it was as if she hovered towards him. He charged forward to meet her halfway. He swung his arm for an attack but she dodged it. Monster was graceful and ever so deadly in his GSK technique, but the woman seemed to know how to defend against it. As he tried to grab and toss her, she countered and kept him off balance. She drove a kick into his knee making it pop. She then swung her body around to dodge him again and hooked his arm around to his back. The woman held his arm behind him and pushed it up. But Monster was too strong and resisted. He tried for a back kick, but he felt it snag between her legs. She twisted her body and slammed him against the wall as he dropped to his knees just feet away from the moaning Circue.

The woman held him down, but Monster proved more formidable. He reached to grab her arm, but instead he felt an impact on the back of his head. His face met with the hard wall, filling the dark hallway with a loud thud. Still conscious, he fought his way to turn and face her. His vision was starting to fade. He fought the urge to black out. He knew something was wrong with him. His head was injured. Monster turned to face her and tried standing but his legs were shaky. He let out a moan as the woman stood above him. He felt his body slip into darkness as the image of her walking away faded to black.

Chapter 14

Now on a higher floor with no crowds to worry about, Reaper was anxious. He could not reach the others over comms and

Phantom seemed to be all too comfortable. He had fallen right into his trap. Reaper bowed his head in shame. Now it was clear. The mission was to stop Phantom and Pandora, Provost's new children. But his mind raced around the thought of their mission; to eliminate the Cleansing Blade. It was not every day that a group of agents were hunted down by another group of agents, all with the same skills, and teacher. Reaper struggled to keep focused, there were only two of them here, and if Provost showed up, at least they would have a chance to stop him here and now.

Phantom stopped and turned to face him, "Now that we have more privacy here, for now, let's talk about how we can sort this problem between us."

"Easy," Reaper showed no fear, "We kill you, take Provost out, and home in time for dinner."

"I love it!" Phantom laughed. "Confidence, skill, tenacity. Everything I was hoping for in the Cleansing Blade. Now enough talking."

Reaper focused. GSK drills raced in his mind. With no weapons, it was time to handle this the old fashioned way. He fixed his sleeves on his collared shirt. Not the comfort of a sneaking suit, but it would have to do. He lunged at Phantom, immediately shooting for offensive tactics. He swiped at him, but Phantom moved his head to dodge it and locked up his other hand with a block. As he countered, Phantom threw Reaper off balance and straight to the floor.

"Want to reassess your approach?" Phantom teased.

Reaper ignored and dashed towards him, they exchanged the strikes of Grab Smash Kill, but no matter how fast Reaper moved; Phantom moved faster. He thrust his hand towards Phantom's face. But Phantom grabbed his wrist and swung him around, smashing him against the wall. Reaper turned to try a spinning back hand, but Phantom caught it. With lightning fast reflexes, Phantom rammed his hand against Reaper's head, driving it into the wall. Reaper fell to the floor, frustrated.

Phantom stepped away and applauded. "Quick, but still lacking, Reaps."

"Reaper!"

He heard Gothica's voice and turned to see her approaching. She was still in her dress, but her crossbow pistol was in hand. Something she was really good at hiding. A quick snap and the arrow flew at Phantom. With little effort, he spun his body and grabbed the flying bolt with his hand. He stopped and picked Reaper up off the floor. Before Reaper could react, he drove the bolt through his shoulder, pinning him against the wall. Reaper curdled from the intense pain searing through his arm. Phantom turned to see Gothica up close and attempt hand-to-hand combat. But Phantom dodged her strikes and grabbed onto her hand. With his other hand he grabbed the bolt from Reaper's shoulder and yanked it out. He spun Gothica and pulled her into a tight choke hold as he kicked Reaper to the ground.

Holding the sharp and bloody arrow against her neck, Phantom clicked his tongue in disappointment, "Now, now. As good as that was. It's time to make a decision, Reaps."

Reaper struggled to his feet, holding his bleeding shoulder, "Don't." He observed Gothica, who was immobilized in a threatening hold. Her face was cold, no sign of fear.

"So, you want to continue and all die? Or I allow the others to live with her sacrifice." Phantom pressed the arrow to barely penetrate her neck.

"You can have me." Reaper looked at him, "Instead of hiding, how about another round?"

"Release her." A soft voice announced behind them.

"Oracle?" Reaper noticed her standing a few yards behind Phantom.

"Look, another to join the party." Phantom released Gothica from his tight hold and flung her to the wall. He promptly drove the arrow through her hand pinning it to the wall.

Reaper felt little assurance as he noticed the beautiful woman from the expo, enter the hall. Pandora, the other member of Provost's new elite team, now stood behind Oracle. "Oracle, behind you!"

Thanks to her psychic abilities, she sensed the woman move to attack. Oracle sidestepped, avoiding Pandora's grab. Oracle turned to face her. Her defensive style was unusual as she stood up straight with her hands down at her side, and dodged Pandora's attacks.

Phantom started laughing, "Hilarious!" He turned to Reaper, "The blind one on the team is the only one that can fight."

Reaper charged at him. The two exchanged punches before Phantom turned, kicking Gothica to the floor and causing her injured hand to pull on the arrow. He locked Reaper's arm up and used the momentum to throw him to the ground. He grabbed Reaper's hair and made him watch as Oracle began to lose the fight.

Oracle backed away towards the others, but Pandora was too fast. She grabbed Oracle and forced her into a rear head lock. Phantom then bent down to grab the arrow from Gothica's hand and pulled it out of the wall, freeing her. He stood up and threw it straight for Oracle's chest. But Pandora caught it just a fingernail's width from hitting Oracle.

"So decision time again, Reapmeister." Phantom walked over Reaper lying flat on the floor. "Who gets to die first?"

"No!" He yelled.

"Stop!" Gothica shouted simultaneously.

Phantom nodded at Pandora who kept silent and nodded back. But Oracle managed to break free and grabbed onto the arrow. Pandora brought her in close and pulled the arrow towards her. Oracle held the arrow, struggling against Pandora's grip as her hands began to shake. Phantom applauded, "Wow, okay, okay. Let her go."

Pandora did as he said and released Oracle. But Oracle felt a chance to attack and spun around to attempt a strike against Pandora's head, but she dodged it easily. She blocked and followed through by forcing Oracle head first into the wall. The impact knocked her glasses off and exposed her blind, marble eyes.

"I'll make you a deal, Cleansing Blade," Phantom began to bargain. "We two, have proven you could be beaten, the Nest could be infiltrated, and even your biggest man could fall to a girl."

Reaper thought about his words. Monster and Circue!

"And that even your Boss could be killed." Phantom walked over to Pandora. "Now, it's your turn. I could easily kill you all here, right now. But where is the challenge in that? I want you to warn the others about us. I want you all to know the names, Phantom and Pandora. It's your turn to chase us."

Reaper struggled to help Gothica. He watched as the two enemies backed away from Oracle still dazed on the floor. Her encounter with Pandora was not easy on her formal clothing. One of her shoes had broken a heel spike and her dress was torn. She sat against the wall struggling to fit her shoes back on. He helped Gothica up and approached her slowly, as Phantom continued back. "Don't worry, we'll be here. As well as Provost, in the Big Apple. Waiting for you." Phantom smiled and took a bow. "I look forward to our next meeting."

With that, the two seemed to glide away. Gothica struggled to place an arrow back in her crossbow, her injured hand trembled as it bled over it. In seconds, the two disappeared down the hallway. Reaper held Gothica up as she planted her stance and nodded to him, "I'm good, check her."

Reaper ran to Oracle who struggled to stand. Trying to find her glasses as she looked down at the floor. He bent down to help her. "Where are you hurt?"

She looked up at him, assurance in her face. "I am fine. Thank you."

"Come on." Reaper helped her to her feet.

She fixed her dress and put her shoes back on. She then bent down to retrieve the glasses. She could tell Reaper was concerned. "I'm okay. Just a bit of a headache. I see you met the ghost."

Reaper took a small breath of relief, "Why didn't you say anything before?" He looked into her eyes before she placed the glasses back on.

"If he disposed of you this quickly, and Boss; then imagine if he was exposed sooner?" She told him.

He knew her point was valid. If Phantom had been found out sooner in the Nest, with his skills, and the possibility of Provost still inside the Nest, it could have been worse. He looked at her and grinned, "Those were some fancy moves." He felt her hand grip his as he held her up. The feel of it was strong but it trembled slightly.

Oracle attempted a grin, "I could read her thoughts a split second before she moved. But then, interference. As if she cleared her head."

Reaper thought about their foes, their moves were faster, minds were sharper. They seemed unstoppable. "I imagine they had training to clear their minds of everything." He assessed her body for injury. "As long as you're okay."

"I think comms are back online." Gothica said as she hobbled over to them, holding her bleeding hand. For a second he thought about the three of them being injured, then Circue and Monster.

"Let's try them." he said, "Monster come in? Circue? Report, both of you." No response. "Come on guys, where are you?" Reaper's voice rose as worry over took him.

Gothica held her uninjured hand to her ear, "I can hear you," she looked at Reaper. "But nothing from them."

Reaper looked at Oracle, "Can you? Can you detect them?" His faith was now purely on her abilities.

Gothica looked slightly confused, "If she can, we should still look around. But not like this." She held up her injured hand, "We need to clean up. No one can see us like this. We'll start a panic."

Reaper knew she was right, "Let's find a bathroom to patch ourselves up."

Oracle moved her head around, but the concussion she suffered made her vision cloudy. "I detect little. The Monster and Circuitcrusher appear to be in a dark narrow passageway."

"Are they alive?" Reaper asked in haste.

Oracle looked at both of them, "I do not know."

Section 3:

The Cleansing

Chapter 15

The humming of the Ark's engines lulled Violet to sleep. Her head rested upon her locker as exhaustion had set in. Dealing with the memories of the Academy, taking care of Boss's remains, on top of moving the team to a distant safe house; it was all so overwhelming. As sleep found her, dreams began to take form. She found herself fading into a familiar night. The dull yellow lights throughout the Academy filled the campus grounds. Violet looked down at her hand, purple colored blood ran down her fingers. She heard Provost call for her, "My sweet Violet." His voice resonated in the night. The others surrounded her in the courtyard.

Uncertainty filled her as she turned to notice Romeo; blood covering his shirt and hands. He stood holding a dagger. She was heartbroken to know that his girlfriend, Julia, had not survived. Violet began to cry in her dream. But Provost's voice was comforting. He told them all that it was the start of something great. He and Boss had helped them to overcome the campus security and escape back into the courtyard. She remembered Provost approaching her. He gently touched her hand and lifted it up to see the wound. His dull gray eyes met hers, "Violet." He had brought them all there for a purpose. Perhaps even destiny. She knew in her heart that all things happened for valid reasons. Some reasons that sometimes, could not be explained. She tried her absolute hardest to find meaning in all she experienced, whether triumph or tragedy. Either way, Violet knew Provost's intentions were good. Or at least, they started off that way.

Her eyes wandered and found Aurora standing under the light post. Light bounced off of her hair, presenting a small aura of colors that hovered above her. If there was ever a time she needed her, it was now. Aurora was always strong. More so than the rest. Though the others were supportive, Aurora helped her get through the hard times during training. She was stoic, and Violet found herself missing her voice. Her dream raced to see her again during a training regimen.

Violet was out of breath, "I can't do it." It was an obstacle course through rivers and dense forest. Three grueling days of survival and endurance training. It was towards the end of the third day.

"You can." Aurora stood above her, breathing heavily. "We all have to make it, or we all fail and start again."

Violet fought for air. "I'm so tired. I can't breathe."

"Get up." Aurora helped her to stand. Violet could not bring herself to respond, "I know you're stronger than this." Aurora looked her in the eyes, "You can do this. You have more fight in you then you know. I can see it." Aurora gave her a comforting smile. "We succeed as a team, or we fail as one."

Violet took heavy breaths as Aurora pulled her along, "Now let's go."

The dream moved to her standing with Aurora and Boss. Aurora hugging her. "I knew you could do this, medic." Violet smiled back. She heard Boss speak, "Great work, Violet. Your medical training is complete." Boss commended. The images of them smiling began to fade. She found herself crying once again.

She tried wiping the tears from her face as Boss' lifeless body lay on the floor of his quarters. His mouth moved, but no words came out. Violet seemed to weep as smoke emerged from his mouth. He seemed to dissolve, but his mouth continued to mumble silent words. Then his voice announced loudly, "There is a problem." Violet ducked and began to shake as the loud words rattled the dream. She met eyes with him one last time, then his raspy voice announced, "Wake up!"

Violet shook out of the dream trembling. She woke to discover her face had wet trails of tears down her cheeks. She shook her head as the red lights of the Ark's cabin brought her back to reality. She looked to see Amraam gaze at her with concern.

"Are you okay?" he asked her. His camouflaged bandana fastened to his head. As if it was part of his armor.

"Yeah," Violet rubbed her eyes, "Bad dreams."

"There's been a problem." Amraam told her.

She looked up with concern, "Oh, what happened?"

"We finally received word from Reaper and Gothica. Monster and Circue are in critical condition."

She rose up from the small bench, "What happened?"

Amraam tried an assuring smile, "They were ambushed. It turns out Dr. Hampton was actually Project Phantom. And part of Provost's new team. They're the ones that killed Boss and nearly killed the others on assignment."

"What's their status?" Violet walked over to the center console.

Romeo spoke in spite, "The two big guys, barely breathing. That's what happens when you go in unprepared and out manned."

Amraam looked over at him, then to Motherboard turning around on the rotating chair near the computer console. She interrupted, "Reaper reported there were only two enemies."

Romeo crossed his arms, "Still. This could've been avoided."

Violet grew tired of hearing Romeo's pessimistic words, "No, it happened that way for a reason. And thank God that nobody else is dead. Those two other agents were obviously skilled enough to take down Monster and the rest."

Romeo kept silent.

She continued, "Did Reaper say what we should do?"

Motherboard responded, "Yes. He said we needed to go back to the Nest, the two need the medical facilities there."

"Things must be bad if that's the case. Let's turn around and get them." Violet ordered.

"Already on course." Motherboard announced, "Estimated arrival time, twenty minutes."

Amraam observed Violet who seemed angry, "Look, Violet's right, these two must be pretty good. They took out five of us."

Romeo snickered, "Yeah, well he also reported it was their mission to bag us. Per orders of our once beloved Provost."

Violet remembered Provost. Once the man that, in a sense, had raised them and trained them day in and day out for years. The man that had them exterminate his old comrades and had now trained a new team to kill them. She was hesitant on accepting that. He could not have possibly wanted that. She looked for good in everything. Even her enemies. And the fact that Provost would betray them and mark them for death, did not add up.

She looked over at Romeo, "If he wants all of us, then he can have us. When we find him, he'll answer for all of this."

Romeo looked at her sharply, "That is for damned sure." With that he walked off.

Violet looked over at Amraam, "Let's hope we can save those two." She could not bear the thought of both Circuitcrusher and Monster dying in the same week as Boss. After all, how was the team supposed to get new gadgets?

"Whew man," Radical spoke up, "I'm getting antsy. This just got deep."

Motherboard shook her head, "I guess we've become obsolete. And it's time to erase us completely."

He walked up to the center console, "Nice puns. I guess we'll need some radical solutions here."

Violet felt some of her stress ease as she chuckled at the cheesy joke. Something she was used to Circuitcrusher doing. If there was ever a time for spirits to pick up, it was now. "Just have faith and we'll make it through this." She tried her best to say something comforting. Though deep down, she worried about her comrades and if they were going to survive.

Chapter 16

The halls of the Nest were filled by the team once again. The aroma of cigarette smoke no longer filled it. The old man that taught them the arts of GSK and stealth was no longer with them. Violet gazed upon his empty quarters. She bowed her head and allowed for a moment of silence. The footsteps of the other team members seemed to fade. Closure was starting to finally make its way into her soul. Boss was put to rest. And hopefully, he would be the only casualty by the hands of this new team. "Violet," She heard Amraam's voice calling to her. She clutched her blond braid tightly, then released as he approached her, "So they're stabilized in recovery." Her gentle green eyes looked up at him, "They're gonna live. But since Circue's spinal cord was severed in the lower vertebrae, he won't be walking anytime soon."

She raised her hand to grip back onto her braid that rested on her shoulder. "At least he's alive. And we got to him in time."

"Monster is okay. You called it too. The small fracture to the back of his skull should be healed soon thanks to your treatment." Amraam could see she was taking the news harder than she appeared to. "He'll be down for a few days at least."

She caressed her hair, "And the others are doing well? I assessed them and they seemed to have minor injuries, but nothing else I missed, right?"

Amraam smiled at her, "You did good. Thanks to you they will all be fine. Gothica's hand is fine, Reaper's shoulder is clean, and Oracle only has the minor concussion."

"That makes me happy." Violet fought a tear forming in her eye. Her emotions were seemingly controllable, but seeing her team broken and battered was discouraging. They were her family. Seeing them hurt only brought her pain. However, it was time to be strong now more than ever.

"Are you doing okay?" Amraam asked as he stepped in closer.

She moved into his arms, feeling his warm embrace. She closed her eyes and buried her face into his chest. Clutching him tightly, it was as if the stress was melting away. Her mind began to feel at ease. Her heart fluttered as she began to feel warm. She pulled away slightly and looked into his eyes. The urge to touch lips was strong and she knew the others were around, but it made no difference. She reached up and pulled him in close. The two kissed for a moment. "Thank you." She whispered as the two slowly backed away from each other.

"Well, that was nice." Amraam smiled. "We should get back to the others, though. I imagine Reaper is planning a strategy on how to track Provost and his new team."

Violet's bright smile broke through her face, "Yes. But first, I need to check on them."

Amraam stopped her, "You look tired. You should get some rest. Especially after three hours in the operating room and the hour flight back here." He noticed her eyes were heavy, but she showed no sign of wear. Her clothes still had blood stains from her treating the others. "A hot shower and rest is what I recommend."

Violet smiled, "Thank you, I will afterwards." She grabbed his hand and stepped towards the infirmary, their fingers gradually interlaced and slowly parted. Amraam smiled back as he watched her leave to check on the others.

She made her way quickly to see Gothica first. Making the turn to her room where she lay resting, Violet noticed her sitting up working out her fingers. "You know you shouldn't move it for a little while. Allow the Adrenaline Solution booster to heal it."

Gothica chuckled, "Don't worry about me, dear. Just stretching it out a bit."

"Is everything else feeling good? What about your elbow?" Violet recalled the x-ray images showing a slight tear in the cartilage from her encounter with Phantom.

"Good," Gothica winked at her, "I'll be ready for another round in no time. Thanks, Violet."

"What were they like? I couldn't see Dr. Hampton being that threatening." Violet asked.

Gothica sighed, "I've never seen a human move like they did. Phantom moved even faster than Oracle. And she's good but he was unbelievable. But the woman, Pandora, she was unreal. I mean, come on, she took out Monster with just her hands, and in a dress."

Violet felt her heart sink. The odds were beginning to stack. "I still don't believe it."

"I didn't either, until I saw them." Gothica stood up, "Then they proved their point."

Violet reached for her hair, "I'm sure Reaper has a good plan."

Gothica smiled at her, "Yeah, he's back to obsessing. So I'm sure he does."

"I'm headed to his room next. Please, Gothica, get some rest." Violet insisted.

"Yes, ma'am."

Violet left the room and proceeded for Reaper's quarters. The thoughts of Phantom and Pandora seemed daunting. But a small bit of hope told her it could not be that horrific. That the two agents were not that powerful. Perhaps, Reaper was more encouraging and she sure hoped so.

The door opened and she saw Reaper lying down and staring at his poster hanging from the ceiling. She looked up at the poster, the aurora borealis over a mountain. A beautiful image. Violet knew the meaning. And if there was ever a time she missed Aurora and the strength she possessed, it was now. "Uh,

Reaper? How's that arm feeling? I trust you've been letting it set?"

Reaper remained still, "Yes, Violet. Thanks to you, we'll be fine."

As their leader, and now that Boss and Provost were no longer around, hearing him say that made her smile. She was appreciated. "You're welcome. I just hope that Circue and Monster recover completely." Reaper kept silent. "But I know we're doing what we can. So, I guess it's out of our hands." Violet approached him slowly. A large bandage wrapped his shoulder. He was wearing a pair of the training pants with no shirt. The wound looked better. No blood showed within the bandage. She thought about the two agents. "Is it true what you said earlier? What Gothica was saying about them, that they surpass us?"

Reaper spoke quietly, "I'm afraid so, Violet. That's why we needed to regroup."

"I think we'll be ready." Violet had faith in her team, "We should have the upper hand, right?"

"Violet, for once I don't know. But I really hope you're right."

She could not believe her ears. He sounded beaten. It was strange to see him like this. She thought of what to say, how to lift his spirits. "I," but she drew a blank. The thought of him falling apart made her uncomfortable. "I hope you get some rest." Violet told him and backed out of his room. The threat seemed too real. They were right about Provost's new team. They seemed unstoppable, and with Reaper having this much doubt, maybe they really were.

Chapter 17

His shoulder was sore. The piercing pain only brought the image of Phantom to mind. Reaper dwelled on these thoughts. That Provost would go against them. Phantom proved to be much more threatening than he fathomed. Was it even possible to beat them? He pulled his arm up to try and flex his arm's muscles. The pain was easing thanks to the Adrenaline Solution treatment.

He heard steps outside of his door creep softly. They were Oracle's, sharp and slow. Reaper sat up in his bed and thought for a second. He was not going to take her words for granted any longer. He shot up and walked to the door. Opening it and seeing her walk down the hall in her leisure attire made him feel a rush. Feeling dizzy, it was getting unbearably difficult to hide his feelings.

"Oracle?"

She stopped in her tracks. Her shorts and sports top were no less attractive than the dress she wore at the expo. "Yes, Reaper?"

"A word please?" She approached and entered his room. Reaper fought to clear his mind. He only wanted to focus on apologizing for his ignorance and the mission that was set before them. Not to mention her withholding the truth about Phantom in the first place because she was protecting them. Now, he could see why.

Oracle navigated the floor easily. He found himself once again entranced by her marble eyes and fiery hair. Her soft voice spoke to him. "Regret, can be a chain all too heavy to carry."

Reaper smirked, she figured him out easily, "Oracle, I'm very sorry. I should've listened to you."

"Only sound minds, can see clearly."

"You have to admit, you can be difficult to understand, though." Reaper tried to get her to speak in "normal" words.

"However, I can see you and hear you without a problem." She stared through him.

Reaper tried to focus. But hearing that made him realize he had been caught by her. Knowing full well she read him like an open book, it was too hard to hide his feelings from her.

"Reaper," She spoke softly and lifted her hand up to cup his cheek. "Running with guilt can only lead to a dark place. Steadfast against it and you will be able to face them."

His heart raced with feelings starting to infringe upon him. "What about, us. I'm sure you can see that. And I am sorry."

She smiled, "Human nature will never be suppressed. No matter how much you run from it."

"Seeing you in trouble, made me realize something. But…" Reaper looked around his room, the door was shut. Only the pounding of his nervous pulse could be heard. He knew that she knew about his feelings towards her. "We can't..."

She caressed his face, "Cannot afford to be human?" She moved her face in closer. Reaper trembled; he had not felt this way in years. Her eyes met his. His thoughts faded from the mission. For once in his life as Reaper, he allowed his emotion to take complete control.

"I'm so sorry, Oracle." He repeated, feeling vulnerable. But she placed her hand gently over his lips. She pulled him in close to embrace as their lips met. Reaper was overwhelmed by the passion that took over. The sounds of the Nest's vents or team members traipsing around the halls, no longer distracted him.

Violet sat in the briefing room. A night's sleep allowed her mind to think clearly. She had hoped the others managed to get sleep. With half of them injured, rest was the best medicine for a faster recovery. Since the daunting mission was coming soon, the team needed to be at their strongest physically. She sipped on her super sweet morning beverage. The sweet aroma of coffee awakened her senses. It was not like she needed it, but just the flavor made the morning ritual another reason to wake up. After being faced with near death, it allowed her to take nothing for granted. Especially, the little things.

The door to the quiet briefing room slid open and Romeo walked through. Violet watched him make his way to grab his cup of coffee. Pitch black and flavorless, she thought. She kept quiet. Knowing he was easy to agitate. Not to mention him having stayed up all night to keep watch on the Nest. Violet kept to herself.

"Sleep well?" He asked her.

Violet was shocked he started the conversation, but she could sense a sarcastic undertone. "Yes. Thank you. And thank you for keeping watch last night."

"Someone's gotta do it." Romeo poured the cup of coffee. "After all, I don't want to wake up to another dead person here."

Violet closed her eyes to think of Boss. "Yes. I don't, either." She thought about Romeo and Julia. Their reminiscing at the Academy seemed to crush his spirits. Now that he initiated conversation, she felt it necessary to speak to him about it. "Romeo, can I tell you something?"

"Oh, boy." Romeo turned around and looked at her as he took a sip, "What?"

Violet kept composed, "I'm really sorry for Julia. I don't know if I ever told you. But what you said a few nights ago at the Academy, that she liked me, I really thought about that." Romeo looked angry. She knew it was a sensitive subject. The likelihood that he had found closure was rare.

"Yeah?" Romeo sipped again.

"And, I think you need to forgive." Violet knew she stepped over his line, but it was too late, "You need to forgive Provost, and that guard that killed her. It was an accident."

"I know what I need."

Violet knew him by now, and what he really wanted. "Death is not the answer, you don't need to pay for her dying and neither does Provost. There is no reason to atone for that sin."

"Everybody gets what they deserve. And as far as I am concerned, Provost has more on his rap sheet than he can pay for."

Her voice raised, "You can't make him pay because you have no right to do so."

Romeo looked at her, "You think men should go unpunished for the horrible deeds they do?"

"No, I believe in two things: All man deserves mercy. And don't judge less you be judged." Violet argued.

He took another sip, "In case you haven't been observing, he ordered another team to kill us. They started with Boss and now want to finish us off."

"And I'm scared, Romeo. I'm terrified." Her voice cracked.

Romeo kept quiet.

"Reaper sounded doubtful. He made it sound like they will."

Romeo grunted, "He just got his ass kicked. We all feel that way when we do."

"No," Violet stood from sitting on the console. "They all feel that way. These two, Phantom and Pandora, beat them all with little trouble."

"Guess we'll wait and see how they handle the rest of us." Romeo sipped from his coffee. The strong flavor cleansed his pallet. It was his favorite drink. He thought of the potential threat they faced and much to his dismay, Violet was right. About everything she spoke. His mind wandered as he stared into his drink. Violet and Julia had once been friends. Even through the hardships of the Academy, they had kept spirits up. Romeo hated the thought of letting go. He wanted revenge against Provost. He wanted to see if it would bring about closure or healing. But Boss had always embedded his philosophy into each of them. Vengeance was for fools.

Romeo did not want to admit it, but Violet was a lot like Boss. Since these new enemies seemed to rattle everyone's cages, they could not turn to Boss for advice. It would never be heard again. Aurora was gone too and her strength and spirit-lifting was buried with her. Violet seemed to be reaching for that torch. He could see uncertainty in her face. He recalled a similar look that Julia had the night she died. And for some strange reason he could not explain, Violet did not deserve to feel that way. She was trying her best and a small amount of sympathy found its way to him. So he tried to think of something comforting, "We'll manage." He said. "After all, have a little faith in us."

Violet broke into a faint smile. Finally, she and Romeo had seen eye to eye. The briefing room door opened and Amraam entered, fitting his bandana as he walked in. Her heart felt warm with the sight of him. He was dressed in his training uniform.

"About to get some morning cardio in to wake up." Amraam moved to stand next to Violet.

Romeo lifted his cup, "Here's mine."

Amraam laughed, "Sorry, I don't do coffee. Stuff makes me too jittery."

"It'll turn you into a warrior." Romeo teased back. "I'll be in there training. I'm surprised Reaper hasn't made his briefing announcement and team pep talk, yet." He walked out of the room.

Amraam looked at Violet, "He has a point. Is Reaper still in bed?"

"He is injured. Although the booster should've healed most of the muscle damage by now. It's been well over twelve hours."

"I'm sure he's fine. Probably pretty tired. He is human, after all. And he hasn't slept in the last few days." He reminded.

She looked at him, "He's scared."

"What do you mean?"

"He told me he was unsure about what to do."

Amraam recalled his military background and training. Under no circumstances were leaders of squads or regiments allowed to show fear, or tell their team they did not know something. If Reaper was telling her this, it could be that maybe things were looking as bad as they seemed. He tried to lift her spirits. "He's probably just shell-shocked and needs some time to think."

Violet looked up into Amraam's dark brown eyes. "Maybe. Because I'm starting to believe him."

Reaper opened his eyes. He had fallen asleep, for the first time in a long time he woke up and felt somewhat refreshed. But he was immediately alerted as a soft hand moved up his chest. His eyes widened and he turned to look at her. Oracle was in the bed with him. He had not forgotten about their night of passion, but it was surreal to him. He took a deep breath and let it out slowly. He grabbed her shoulder and pulled her in as she turned to lay on him.

"I trust sleep was unable to elude you this time." Oracle spoke quietly. Her whisper was comforting.

"Yeah," He was still not fully aware of what had happened. He did not want to forget about it, but he did not want to think about it too much either.

"You seem to have more on your mind. Doubt still plagues it." She moved her hand and gently caressed his arm and wounded shoulder.

Reaper smiled, "There's no hiding from you is there?"

"You have tried before."

He felt embarrassed as she found him out. "Yeah, that's true." He let out a breath, "I don't know. After seeing what Phantom can do, and Pandora when she had you. I'm honestly not sure if we can do this."

"You must purge yourself." Oracle said.

He knew she was going to start giving him advice, but he would still have to decode it. "How?"

"Acceptance of who you are. You are still human, Reaper."

"I don't want to be sometimes."

"But even your foes, are still only human." her voice spoke softly.

Reaper thought about it, "You're right, they are. But I've seen people do amazing things in both good and evil. And if we fail, Provost can destroy everything."

"You're role serves you well. But you will infect the others as they follow."

He thought about the words she spoke, he was trying to get into the right frame of mind. She then left his side and slid out of the bed. "Allow me to get ready. A new day."

He stood up in the bed. "Oracle," He tried to stop her as she proceeded to his door. She turned to look at him, "Thank you." He said. She left the room. He wondered if the others had figured out he was running late in the morning. It was going to be difficult to make it to the showers without anyone seeing him traipse the hallway. He hoped no one had seen Oracle make her way out of his room.

Now, the hallway was clear, and he snuck to the showers. His hand pushed the door open and revealed Gothica combing out her hair. He felt as if he was caught red handed. Ready for a lecture. But Gothica seemed better, "Sleeping in, eh?"

Reaper looked at the clock above the door of the large bathroom, "It's only seven. I'm not that late am I?"

"No," Gothica turned and teased, "Just not used to you being last in here is all."

He walked over to one of the sinks and ran the water until it got hot. "Just making sure this shoulder heals okay. How's the hand?"

Gothica twisted her hand and flexed her fingers. "It feels much better today. This booster stuff is really nice to have."

"I wouldn't get used to it. Takes a while to make, and since Circue is down for a while, we won't be seeing much in the next few weeks."

"You'd be surprised," Gothica looked over at him as he washed and proceeded to shave the small amount of hair on his face. "He's actually awake. Seems okay, he's still doped up on medicine from being in the recovery tank for twelve hours."

The steam of the hot water fogged up the mirror, but he continued to shave, "Good. I hope he's back in action sooner then." He thought about Oracle's advice. If anyone knew what she meant and how to help him, it was Gothica. "Can I ask you a question?"

"Shoot."

"Oracle told me, uh," He caught himself. "Yesterday, something about me fitting my role, but infecting the others. And I'm trying to understand her more." He sounded disappointed, "She was right about Phantom. I just couldn't see it."

She finished with her hair. The bright lights allowed the fading dye in her hair to be more noticable. "Okay. So your role would mean." She thought for a second. "Member of an elite group. The leader? And if that's the case, you're infecting others. You did seem really discouraged yesterday."

Reaper thought about it. Oracle had made sense. It just took another mind to help him see. "Yeah, that's it." His eyes raced around the mirror, as if he were searching for the clue. "Violet!"

"What, what about her?"

He vaguely remembered her coming into his room to check on him. He did not feel like discussing the mission, and then Violet seemed to be very disheartened by the end of the conversation. "I think I told Violet something I shouldn't have."

"That is?"

"I told her, I didn't know what to do." Reaper looked at the running water. He felt shame for demoralizing his team. "Oracle said I was fit to lead, but I can infect the rest with doubt if I show it."

Gothica looked at him, "She's right. You should know better than to doubt anything, let alone show it. And Violet is just trying to motivate us. I imagine she's been struggling to keep up with all of the injured and medical treatment. She's worn out, too."

"I may have let her and some of the others down."

"Reaper," Gothica's tone was serious, "You should know you can't show weakness. Not to your enemies, and certainly not to your own team. You have to know we will follow you into hell if we had to and you need to see that. Everyone is counting on you as much as you need to count on all of us. We're a team."

Reaper rinsed his face off. The water dripped from his nose and chin as he watched the droplets fall down the drain. "You're right. Oracle was right. And if we're to beat this," He looked at her with confidence, "We need to do it as the team we once were."

Chapter 18

The briefing room was quiet. All were awaiting the start of Reaper's mission briefing. Each of the team wore their leaner sneaking suits. Still able to deflect and handle damage done to it accordingly, it allowed for faster movement, more versatile in the field but with limited carry capacity. This meant that the team member needed to rely on more skill. Words of wisdom passed on that Boss had drilled into their minds, "The best skill still beats the best tool." Not to mention the leaner suit gave for more advanced gadgets. Such as the flexible mission pad screen. Though, the major technological advancement of the suit was still in death. The suit remained biosynthetic. Dissolving both itself and the team member that died in it. A brutal truth that lingered in the back of their minds. One that would stay with Violet forever.

Violet observed Reaper placing his hands on the center console. Her eyes wandered as she looked behind him, expecting to see Boss or smell a wisp of his smoke cloud. They were on their own now. No elder's guidance before being sent to battle. It was left for Reaper to lead them. She looked to see Gothica standing at the end of the row, her experience as a former CIA agent and background was insightful. And at least she helped to fill the seat of wisdom. Violet stroked her braid until she felt Amraam's hand grip hers through their gloves. She nonchalantly gripped his back as she released her braid.

She turned to see the others ready. Only the three giants were missing. One was on another mission, and the other two in the infirmary healing from their last battle with Provost's new team. A battle she would encounter soon. She took a second to observe the others. Romeo seemed to have his dagger in place; along his left arm, with a customized sheath that allowed him to still be flexible enough to fight efficiently. The word 'Live' inscribed in the blade. Hopefully, he would allow Provost that mercy. Violet looked over at Radical tugging on his detonation cord bracelets he had wrapped around his wrists. Thanks to Circue, they were a convenient way to drop high explosives quickly. Not to mention, Radical had acquired more refined explosive devices from Circue; as he fondled one of them in his hand. A shaped sticky charge, dubbed 'cannon bombs' with the ability to blow out in certain directions. Motherboard stood next to him. Her glasses were secured on her face, the lenses adjusting to the light in the room. She let go of the large custom pad and moved to the more suitable 'Flex-Screen' system Circue had worked on fitting to her sneaking suit. Violet was curious as Motherboard was definitely warming up to Radical's charm. After all, the two seemed to spend quite a bit of time together both in the Nest and in the field.

Violet's eyes then found Gothica. She admired her for her experience and knowledge. Even her skills were up to par. And her shorter hair complemented her facial features. The only thing Violet remained uncertain about was why Gothica insisted on carrying a crossbow pistol. It was her weapon of choice, but had slow reloading capabilities and limited ammunition. She figured the silent feature was most important. Her eyes wandered a little further and landed on Oracle. A strange woman that Reaper had recruited only a few months prior. Violet remained unsure what he saw in her at the time, but when it came to training and her ability to adapt, Violet was intrigued. Oracle's abilities to see despite being blind were baffling. But she was difficult to understand. There was something about her that made Violet unsure. She found her bizarre personality and speech to simply be a trait of her disability. And for some reason, being around her made Violet feel slightly uncomfortable.

Violet turned and looked back at Amraam, still holding her hand. His camouflaged bandana sat on his head perfectly as if it was a part of him. He looked back at her and winked. His assuring signal to her allowed her to keep the faith in her team and their mission to come. Then Reaper spoke.

"Okay team, listen up. First, I want to apologize for what I've done." He looked over at Violet, "I never meant to cause uncertainty amongst us. And I thank you all for staying by my side. We've seen too much this last week. Boss, Provost's new team, and our own injured and crippled. I don't want that to distract us from what we have to do." He moved his attention to Oracle. A smile emerged on his face. "Oracle has allowed us a great advantage. And if we listen to her closely, we can gain a tactical advantage on our foes."

Romeo chuckled and shook his head, "Perhaps her insight is what's getting us into trouble."

Reaper turned to him, "What do you mean?"

Romeo crossed his arms, "Well, since she's been here, we've encountered far more trouble and death while following her visions."

"What are you saying?" Reaper ordered in defense.

"She's the third. How do you not see that one?" Romeo grew agitated. "The third one from Project Phantom and Pandora that supposedly died."

Violet's stomach was in knots. Romeo had felt it too. She sensed Oracle was unusual, and having Romeo call it, only made her see it more.

She watched Reaper stumble over his words, "The third was shown dead on the data and HE was cremated."

"And who told you that?" Romeo insisted, "Dr. Phantom?"

Reaper kept silent.

"You keep defending her as if she's helped us. She's only set us up. The Academy. The art expo. She's responsible for Monster and Circue. She led you guys to the slaughter. And you know what? I would say she killed Boss." The room was silent. Not even the sounds of breathing could be heard.

Reaper broke the silence, sounding unconfident, "No. She's with us. Not them…"

"Wait a minute," Romeo observed Reaper's shyness, "You like her." He spoke in spite. "You have feelings for her?"

Violet could feel her eyes water as Reaper bowed his head in shame. Her leader was once again broken. The team was once again broken.

Oracle stepped up to speak, "There is a great crack within the blade. And it must be cleansed."

"Shut up!" Romeo snapped. "We should just kill you right now. Then we'd only have the two and the scumbag. How's that for cleansing. Getting rid of the infiltrator among us."

Oracle moved her head as if to read him, "Julia," She paused. Romeo grew angry. "She is fighting to escape."

Romeo walked towards her, stricken by her words. The blind woman continued, "She cries to leave where you have kept her."

Romeo began pulling out his dagger, "Don't." He glared at her.

"Had you not killed her, she would be free."

"I'm warning you."

Violet stepped forward and grabbed on to Romeo's arm, Amraam close behind her. "What is she talking about?" Violet was losing hope. And now, Oracle's words were piercing her.

Oracle was not on the mission at the Academy, nor did she have any knowledge of Julia. Violet repeated, "Romeo, what is she saying?"

Romeo kept his glare on Oracle.

Oracle continued to move her head, looking around the room as if past scenes played out in front of her. "The dagger you carry imprisons you. Her blood is on your hands."

Violet watched on, seeing Oracle and Romeo stare each other down, making him seem frail. Violet tried to interpret. She, too, had told Romeo about forgiving himself. Julia's death being an accident, but this was different. Oracle pointed out one crucial detail. And by the look of it on Romeo's face, she was right.

The bizarre woman spoke, "The blade that you carried entered her body."

Violet tried piecing it together; Romeo told them she had died that night, and that he was to blame. But now, it was clear, Julia's death was not by the guard, but by Romeo himself. She died because Romeo had killed her. With his dagger! She figured it out and hesitated, "Romeo, you killed her? Is that true?"

Romeo's face tried hiding the guilt, but it was starting to show.

Oracle looked at him, "But it was not your fault. So why punish, when still innocent?"

"Romeo, please?" Violet pleaded as she felt his arm tense. The words of the mysterious woman were starting to make sense. "Say something. Is it true?"

Romeo barely spoke, "Yes."

She could tell he was struggling.

"I killed her." He said.

The team was silent. Violet could not believe it. After all these years, he had held that inside of him. Hatred, for himself.

"Oh, God." Violet clung on to him tighter. "But it was an accident."

Oracle looked deeper into Romeo's eyes, "Guilt, is stacked high on your shoulders. Truth, will carry on."

Violet could feel Romeo easing up. Then he opened his mouth. "I killed her. She fell on top of me when the guard pushed her. I was still holding the knife. I didn't know until it was too late."

Reaper walked up to them, "Why didn't you say anything before?"

Violet chimed in, "Forgive yourself, Romeo. Please."

Romeo looked around, "I couldn't. I couldn't let it go. You wouldn't either."

Oracle spoke to him, "The blade carries your last promise to her. But you failed your promise."

"What?" Romeo felt weak.

"Her message. To 'Live' on." Oracle said. "Julia can stay in your heart, but she must be freed from your grasps."

Violet struggled with the thought of Romeo's accident, "Romeo, please." She looked at Oracle, she was starting to make sense. "Listen to her."

Gothica took a deep breath before speaking, "Romeo, Oracle is right, you say you killed her when you didn't. You did not kill her on purpose. You have to let that go."

He stood quiet.

Violet tried to reason, "You promised her." She told him.

She triggered his memory, the last night at the Academy. Julia asked him to promise her to live. But she died before she could say more. "Julia," Romeo whispered. "She did not deserve it."

Oracle set her hand on his shoulder, "And neither did you." She stopped and backed away from him.

Violet could feel him starting to relax. It was starting to make more sense. The reasons for the word 'live' on the blade.

Romeo looked down at the floor, shocked that she read the truth from his mind. Something he had hidden away for years. Something that no one had ever known but him.

Oracle spoke more, "The blade you carry, still has her blood, and the blood of others that you love."

"I just need the blood of Provost across it." Romeo mumbled.

Oracle froze, then shifted her head back, "And you will, but the blade you carry will carry more than just the blood of the Provost. The blood of your team will also share the blade."

Violet felt a chill. "Trust us, Romeo. Don't turn on us."

Romeo turned to face Violet. "I would never."

She pleaded, "Julia wants you to let her go. For all of our sake."

Romeo struggled to speak, but no words came out.

Violet looked at Reaper for assurance. "What do we do?" She felt nothing but absolute dread as the team seemed to be falling apart.

Reaper looked around the room. The team seemed lost. Boss would have been disappointed in them. Oracle now made him nervous. Romeo's accusations towards her made him think about it. And would Romeo really use his knife to stab them all in the back? As their leader, he was speechless. He fought within himself to find the words and take charge of the derailing team. He bowed his head down for a second and then looked around to see his team. They all looked at each other and then back at him. As if they were looking for him to have the answer. But could they see that he was tired? He shut his eyes again. A strange voice then fluttered through his mind. He recognized it as Aurora's. His mind recalled a conversation of theirs.

"You know they depend on you right?" Aurora told him. *"Leading us to this camp? You can't just change plans on us like before."*

"If it means getting intel on this Pat Zamora, then I will do better." Reaper responded.

"Well, he could be there." Aurora warned. *"And if he is, you need to maintain your composure this time."*

"I'll do my best." Reaper told her.

"Your best? I laugh at your best." Aurora teased and smiled at him, *"Do it for your team. And if this helps; do it for me…"*

Reaper snapped out of it. Aurora's words echoed. "For her." Reaper looked around the room to see them all still staring at him. It was time to take charge. He inhaled and placed his hands upon the center console. "Romeo, let Julia go."

Romeo looked back at him, "Why? Provost had no regard. Both of them trained us to move past it, but you can't just move past it."

Reaper recalled Boss and his conversation just a few days ago, "I know Provost may have pushed us, Boss told us to train and to forget about the past. And maybe they were right at that time. But you have to accept it first, before you can move on." Romeo looked as if he struggled with the concept. "And because, we need you for this." Reaper said. "Now, the task in front of us may be daunting. And we can do this, but only if we are a team." He nodded to Violet. Violet felt her faith returning. Reaper was taking charge to lead them into battle.

"Provost must be apprehended and his team of two must be dealt with. Phantom likes to play games. He said he enjoyed a challenge and made it clear that their mission was to put an end to us. That means our mission objective," Reaper looked at Romeo, "Is to live, and not allow them the satisfaction." Romeo looked down then back up at him.

Violet felt comfort in Reaper's words. She knew he had been wrong to doubt. She could feel the faith in her team and morale improving slowly. She was not a fan of violence to combat violence, but when she saw Monster and Circue in the shape they were in, it was clear. These enemies were not going to stop.

Reaper waved for Oracle to approach the console, "Now I've talked with Oracle about where to start looking." Reaper looked at her. His feeling for her remained, but a shadow of doubt against her existed now.

Oracle seemed to look at him. "I do not ask that you all trust me." She stated, "But I do ask to cleanse yourselves of doubt. Provost's new team is strong. Pandora was more than we could handle."

Reaper defended, "And if she could break Monster and Circue," He looked at her, "Then we all need to watch out for one another." He looked around. Few nodding back at him. "But first, we need to find them. Phantom said they would be waiting for us somewhere in New York City. And Oracle has come up with a few possibilities." He directed her to start.

Oracle remained still and silent, her head swayed back and forth. "I see the city. I see the Phantom hiding amongst a hollow land."

Romeo spoke up, "So a park, cold and dead?"

Violet was surprised by him, he spoke to help and not to argue.

Oracle continued, "This Phantom walks along the levels of the man-made forest."

"Not a park," Amraam chimed in, "The city, but a part of it that's not thriving? It's New York, it's always thriving."

Gothica had an idea, "Levels? A building?"

Violet was pleased to see the team working together. Putting their faith in a woman they did not understand nor fully trust, but had just shown them proof to do so.

"A hollow building?" Radical joined in, "Let me think about some of the buildings there and their names for a second."

Motherboard looked at him and laughed, "You're thinking way too hard. A hollow building sounds like an empty building. Construction maybe?"

Reaper looked around, seeing his team in action once again, "That's good Motherboard. Start looking into new developments in the city."

"Already on it." Motherboard stretched out her flex-screen pad and researched the city.

Reaper placed his finger to his ear, and grinned, "I have a surprise for us, someone wants to key in." He looked over to the computer screen that was set above the console hologram of New York City. As it faded, Circuitcrusher's face displayed on the screen.

"Hello all." He chirped as his large blue eyes seemed to wander off. He appeared to be groggy from the recovery tank's anesthesia. "I wanted to wish you all good luck." he slurred.

Violet's smile lit up to see him alive and well. "Great to see you awake."

Radical chuckled, "And a little happier than usual, eh Circue?"

"The sedatives and Adreeenaline Solution boooster." He exaggerated the E sound as he spoke, "Are working wonders at the moment." He looked lost as the screen would zoom into his eye.

"Are you feeling okay?" Gothica asked.

"I have weird dreams about that woman. I feel like I'm right there in the hallway with her. Lady gave me the creeps. She was like a shadow that just stood there and hovered around. I've never seen anything like it."

Romeo thought about what Circue had just described. "A shadow? Hovering." He recalled his encounter at the Academy. "She was there." he whispered.

"What?" Violet asked.

"The Academy," he said as the team turned to look at him, "That woman was there. That's who I saw in the dorms with me, and then again at the admin building. That's who gave us the P markings on our necks."

Violet linked the two stories from him and Circue together. And she did not like that they were connected. "They watched us the whole time." Romeo stepped back. The realization must have hit him finally. Violet watched as he looked down to the floor. She could tell he realized the threat was more than he expected.

Unfazed by the conversations and questions from the team, Circue babbled on, "But I do have some gadgetsss for you to take. First is the Cat-Eye part deux. It has the same features like the glasses but without wearing glasses." He dropped the screen and picked it upside down. "And then there's the new flex screen pads on your sneak…wait, no I already said that. Those are old." He was lost again. "You're familiar with their standard vision modes, but I talked with Motherbeed, and came up with a new feature." Circue coughed, "Since they cut comms last time, I added to the Cat-Eyes something that will keep track of you all, and in sync with the Cat-Eyes part deuces." Some of them laughed at his expense, but Circue remained unfazed as he slurred away, "Marking you each with a signal that will allow you all to see each other in real time, granted you turn them on or off via the flex pad."

"Thanks, Circue," Reaper acknowledged, "Now get some rest."

The screen went black. Violet started to regain confidence. The team was back on track and the mission was clear. But Reaper and Oracle were not finished yet.

"Anything else you can see, Oracle?" Reaper asked.

Her head was still and her marble colored eyes wandered the room. "Levels, three joined at the bottom."

"Got it." Motherboard announced, "A new building, forty stories tall. Three sections. It's the future sight of the Alan Frey Enterprises."

"Then that's where we start." Reaper agreed. "Are we close?"

Oracle turned to him and smiled, "I have found the way, now it's your turn."

Reaper nodded, "Okay team. If we're going to do this, we need to be one unit. As of now, I am officially disbanding Shadows of the Sun. Phantom wanted the Cleansing Blade, so he'll get it. But most of all, for Boss." He stopped for a second, "May he rest in peace." Reaper stood up straight and looked at his team. "I hereby reinstate the Cleansing Blade."

Section 4:

The Hollow

Chapter 19

The city that never sleeps contained within it the two named after the haunter of nightmares and hell bringer of man. Both being lead by the creator of the Cleansing Blade. The smell of city smog and ocean breeze filled the air. Though it was the middle of the night, the city glowed with all of light bouncing off the clouds above. Cars racing and horns honking in the distance. Little traffic drove through the developing block. The construction area was just a few blocks down. Three buildings linked by a first level entrance center. Just as Oracle had depicted it, it was the bones of the large scale building. Spread out throughout the plot of land. Some floors had drywall up and certain parts were more developed than others, like windows and roofing on two of the towers. The building lay there still, quiet in the middle of the hollow lot.

Violet moved quickly to close the gap between her and Romeo. Reaper had instructed that they divide into smaller teams to swarm the area and keep a watch from all angles. After crossing the Hudson River, it was just a few more blocks down to the complex. Walking deeper into the dark streets, Violet could see the building coming up just past an apartment complex. She found herself missing Amraam already. He was ordered to stay with Oracle when they infiltrate the building. Violet was allowed to go with Romeo since she seemed to understand him, and since she was the only one on the team that he could tolerate at the moment. They needed a vantage point. So their objective was to get to the roof of the apartment building and watch for any suspicious activity. Understanding full well that this team and Provost knew how to utilize stealth, it was going to be a game of cat and mouse. As many eyes on the area as possible would improve the attempts at taking the enemies down.

She stayed close to Romeo as he pulled out a small pick for the lock on the apartment's side entrance. It was going to be tricky navigating the hallways of an occupied building full of innocent people. She thought about what would happen if they failed, Provost was capable of horrific things. And she thought of what would happen to all of the people in the building. Let alone the city.

"Would you focus?" Romeo interrupted her thoughts.

"Sorry." Violet looked around, "Got it open? Now how do you want to get to the roof?"

"We'll split up." Romeo looked up. "I'll take the far stairs, you take these." He pointed to the staircase nearby.

Violet nodded, "We'll meet on the roof?"

"Yeah,"

"Be careful." She said softly.

Romeo turned back at her, "You too."

Violet grinned at him, "Remember to turn on the tracker to keep tabs on each other. I should be able to see you through this building."

Romeo simply nodded.

Violet watched as Romeo snuck down the hallway. The dented walls and dirty floor filled the stale stairwell. Violet looked up to see the stairs spiral up towards the top. She kept close to the walls and proceeded carefully. She was silent in her approach. Careful not to wake up any of the occupants. Running into any of the enemy alone could prove fatal. Then she walked up on a man lying down in the stairway. She could tell that he was still alive, but breathing irregularly. Her instinct was to help him. She got closer and noticed he was bleeding across his cheek. She looked closely, the blood trails led to the symbols, P vs CB. Her heart sank. She recognized the writing. It was the same as seen on their necks and the walls of the Academy. Provost and the others were certainly here and toying with them. Violet bent down to check the man's pulse. He appeared to be alive, but unconscious.

Violet looked around the area. She checked her wrist pad to make sure the Cat-Eye was on and filtering the images of her team. The others were probably too far away. She scanned the walls and saw a small glowing silhouette of Romeo moving quickly up the stairway. She needed to make time and cover more ground. Throwing caution to the wind, she reached for her auto pistol. She froze when she felt nothing and looked down at her holster. Her weapon was missing. The threat became real, and she could feel her nerves firing with terror. She looked around with her Cat-Eye scanner to locate Amraam anywhere, all she could see were spots on the HUD that indicated the others. Then the lights in the stairwell flickered. And a loud screech resonated from outside. She looked up and saw a figure looking down at her just two floors up. The lights blacked out for a second and returned to normal.

Violet knew it was one of them. Pandora, more than likely, since that's what the others had reported noticing. She ran up the stairs quickly but could see nothing. Then on the wall next to her, she spotted the same symbol. She looked up and saw only three more floors until the top. Figuring that if she ran into trouble this close to the top, Romeo would be closer to aide.

She reached the top floor and flung the door to the hallway open. Running through it, she managed to catch a glimpse of Romeo walking towards her. Relief filled her for a moment as she walked towards him. A cold breeze hit her cheek. It felt as if water was on her face. She moved her hand up to wipe her cheek and looked at her glove. Purple blood. She stopped and quickly turned around. Nothing. Then she turned back to see Romeo standing on guard next to her. Startled, she let out a quiet gasp.

Romeo noticed her face, "How'd this happen?"

"She's here." Violet said, "I think Pandora is here."

He scanned the area, but saw nothing. Then the same sound and the lights flickered. He pulled her in close. The two of them scanned the area for another chance to spot the figure. Violet kept her eyes open but saw nothing. She turned and felt Romeo pull her again, then the two turned to face down the hall. Just a few yards away, they spotted the figure standing there. The lights faded then went to black. Romeo reached for his sidearm and dagger. The lights returned to normal, but only his dagger was in his hand. "What the?"

Violet looked at him to see that his pistol was missing. "No, how? Where is she?"

Romeo checked his placement, no other equipment was missing. Just his M9.

Violet swallowed her lump of fear. "She disarmed us." She moved forward but stopped to pull Romeo to face her. "Let me check you real quick." She looked at his face, no blood, no sign of anything on him. "Okay, she only tagged me, I guess."

Romeo looked at the slice, "How'd she do that? Disarmed us without us knowing?" He shook his head but attended back to her face. "It's just a small cut. She's playing with us." A sound of a door closing caught their attention. "And there she is."

Violet moved towards the sound with Romeo on her tail. They turned the corner and spotted a hatch that led to the roof. "I think she wants us to follow her."

"Gotta get up there anyway." Romeo secured his dagger in its sheath. "I'll go first."

She nodded and held her braid tightly. The two climbed up the narrow staircase and made it to the hatch. Romeo checked to see it was still unlocked and proceeded through slowly at first. No sign of any tripwires or traps, and no legs within the immediate vicinity. Romeo leaped out of the hatch and onto the roof.

Violet wiped her face again and leaped out right after him. The two swept the area but no signs of Pandora anywhere.

"She's good at disappearing." Romeo grunted.

Violet saw the building just beyond them, "Let's hope she's not as good at fighting."

"Wonder why they haven't tried to kill us yet." Romeo turned back, "She let you live." He looked at her cheek.

"Maybe Provost ordered them to show some mercy for us?" Violet hoped.

Romeo grinned at her, "Don't hold your breath."

The two walked over to the edge carefully and took cover behind a large ventilation duct. They both observed the hollow building that lay before them. A large structure with plenty of hiding spots. Violet scanned the area with her Cat-Eye. She noticed the others slowly making their way to the tower. Some, closer than others. A high fence sectioned off the sight. She checked the area, no sign of any movement. It was difficult to comprehend someone with that much stealth ability.

She watched as Romeo reached into his vest pouch and pulled out a small scope to view the area closely. Their suits were leaner, and still gave them enough storage compartments to have all the basic gear. Through their training, Boss would instill that skill beats any gadget in the field. She thought about him. The old man trained them in the very essentials of combat and sneaking. For years, they learned new skills from Boss and Provost. They were the best teachers in the world. She snapped out of her thoughts for a second to see Romeo standing up.

"What do you see?" Violet alerted.

Romeo lowered the scope, "I see somebody."

"Who?"

"They're sitting down." Romeo concentrated.

Violet tried to pinpoint the angle of his scope to where he was scanning, locating the person sitting down. She looked back at Romeo, "Anything?" She was getting excited, so excited that she was starting to forget to keep an eye out on their location.

"Report, Romeo?" Reaper's voice ordered. "Are you on the roof?"

"Affirmative." Violet responded instead. "We've located a person sitting in the building. Not sure, no positive ID yet."

Reaper sounded alerted, "We've made it to the north tower. We're going to work our way up then we'll....."

Comms cut to silence. Romeo looked over at Violet for a second, "What happened?"

Violet tried reaching him, "Reaper, what did you say?"

No response.

"Reaper? Amraam?!" Violet panicked. "Hello?"

Romeo looked at his wrist pad, "Comms are down. But nothing else."

Violet looked up at him, "What does that mean?"

Romeo continued to view the subject on the chair. "It means we're close."

"They could be trying to block our comms." Violet took a deep breath. Romeo remained still. "What is the plan?" He said nothing. Violet could hear his gloves gripping the scope tighter. "Hey, what is it?"

"I see him." Romeo mumbled.

"Who?"

"The one in the chair."

Violet paused for second, Romeo was fixated on them, "I know that. Who is it?"

Romeo took a second to respond, then looked back at her, "Provost."

Chapter 20

Reaper approached the first floor of the northern tower. Comms appeared to be down, again. He slapped his wrist pad. "Violet? Radical?" He looked at Gothica who stayed low as they were about to enter the construction site. "They've knocked out our comms again."

Gothica remained alert, "Well that's good news."

Reaper was puzzled, "How?"

"This must be the right building. Guess we just rely on sight then. We still have the ability to track everyone using the lens."

"You're right." Reaper looked back up the tower. "Let's move up. See if we can find that individual they mentioned. Could be a hostage, so be extra cautious."

Gothica cocked back her crossbow pistol, "Right behind you."

Reaper and Gothica made it to the empty stairwell. Some levels were more complete than others. More so in the middle floors. Reaper watched as Violet and Romeo's tracers were making their way up the southern tower. He turned back at

Gothica, "Let's get up to a good vantage point." She nodded and the two made their way up another flight of stairs. The ground was now far below. And the random loud screech in the background drowned out the city's humming momentarily.

Reaper thought about having his hi-cap pistol drawn. If people noticed them, the police department would swarm the area. And from there, only God knows what Provost or Phantom would try to pull. He noticed the small number on the column as the two made it to another floor. Level 27. It would be high enough. Due to the floor being walled and windowed already, it would provide some cover as they overlooked the other two wings. He looked through his Cat-Eye to see the two signals make their way to the southern wing. Romeo and Violet appeared to be working their way up slowly. Was something wrong?

He found himself worrying about their plan. Then more thoughts clouded his mind. He thought more about the ones who had homes still in the world outside of the Cleansing Blade. Crosshair still with his father. Gothica was as tenacious as she was smart. Her mentorship was invaluable to him. But he could not help but feel that he had led them all to their doom. Was Provost really going to have them killed? And was Phantom going to carry out the orders? He did not want to think about the other, Pandora. Just the thought about Monster and Circue made him nauseous.

Gothica interrupted his thought, "They'll be fine. Slow and steady, not sure why we were in a hurry."

Reaper turned to her and was about to speak until he saw the symbol P vs R behind her. His eyes glared at the symbol for a second.

"What is it?" Gothica turned to notice it. "Oh, never mind. Guess we're in the right building."

Reaper drew his pistol, "Keep your eyes open." The two stepped back and made their way down the narrow hallway. The city lights pierced through windows from the offices being constructed. The two operatives approached a small door where another symbol was carved into it. He took a deep breath and carefully opened it with his pistol drawn.

The hallway continued and more office development branched from it. The coast was clear for now, but Reaper knew better, Phantom liked games and the symbols were like breadcrumbs. The two crept slowly until Reaper caught sight of a tall figure standing before him. He held his pistol tight and aimed it at the silhouette. Then it moved towards him slowly and spoke, "Welcome back, Reaps."

"Phantom." Reaper held his stance. Gothica stood next to him at the ready.

"Glad you all made it." Phantom's face appeared as the lights from the city slowly grazed across it. His face and hazel eyes appeared like a ghost's face against the dark sneaking suit that he wore. It was somewhat familiar to their old style. Lean and able to deflect a fair amount of gun fire as long as the hit was not direct. But Phantom wore no vest, and it appeared he had no weapons on him. Phantom pointed at them, "Why don't you put the guns away. After all, one shot and the whole division of police will show up." He shrugged, "Then who knows what will happen." A grim smile appeared across his face.

"You wanted us," Reaper said, "And only us, the Cleansing Blade."

"Very good." Phantom applauded, "Provost always did talk highly of you. And your astounding ability to not know when to quit."

Reaper kept focused, he could hear Gothica breathing next to him still. He began to worry. Could they take him on?

"But I am disappointed in our last encounter. You all appeared to be lousy fighters. So I guess now we can make it fair and I'll let you have the first hit. What do ya say, Reaps?"

Reaper knew what he had to do. Selfish, but necessary. He spoke to Gothica, "Go."

"What?"

"Leave," Reaper repeated. He turned to look over at her, "That's an order."

"You can't take him on alone. Are you serious?" She sounded angry.

"Find the others. Regroup on Romeo's position." He told her.

"I'm not leaving you here." She insisted.

"Alice." He snapped. "Please, I'll take care of this."

She appeared to be shocked at his comment. He had committed a direct violation of the team. No names. She looked uncertain, "Come back to us."

Reaper nodded, "Go!" He watched her as she turned to leave out the door and head down the stairs. He holstered his pistol. He turned to face Phantom and the two locked eyes.

"What a true gentleman." Phantom bowed at him. "I must admit, as polite as that was, I'm astonished you don't want help."

Reaper kept is eyes on his target, sizing him up once again. "You said you wanted the battle of your dreams. Well, I guess the Grim Reaper is here, and found the Dark Phantom."

Phantom laughed, "Yes, indeed he did."

"Then let's settle this." Reaper charged at him. Running the advanced moves of Grab Smash Kill through his mind, he would need all the help from his training.

The two collided. Reaper moved as fast as his body would allow, but Phantom countered every move. After just a few seconds, he could tell Phantom anticipated every move. Reaper tried mixing up his strikes to throw Phantom off, but to no avail. He tried for a sharp strike to his neck. Phantom grabbed his hand and threw him hard through a side wall.

"Come on, Reaps! I want more!" Phantom shouted.

Reaper shot up, ready for another round. He held his hands up and moved to attack once again. Phantom sidestepped and struck him in the chest, shoving him back down. Reaper shook his head. He would not quit as long as Phantom stood. He rolled back up and leapt to strike his foe down. But Phantom was too fast and sidestepped again, smashing Reaper across the back. Reaper did not miss a beat and swung around to barrage Phantom again. He grabbed Phantom's arm, holding it tightly and made an attempt to back hand his face. Phantom blocked and reversed the hold, turning Reaper around again.

"Takes two, to tango." Phantom cheered.

Reaper growled and performed a textbook perfect spinning back hand. But his hand only met air. He turned around and saw Phantom standing back, then leapt at him. Reaper found himself on the defensive as Phantom bombarded him with lightning fast blows to his midsection and face. Reaper felt a fist across his head. He ducked down to perform a trip to slow Phantom down, but he jumped over it and kicked Reaper in the head. He fell back and rolled to fighting stance. His vision was blurring from the hard blows to the head. Phantom did not appear winded or injured.

Reaper let out a grunt in frustration, "Come and get me."

Phantom's eyes lit up with excitement, "Rejoice Reaper! I'll allow you live to see the end of your team."

"No!" Reaper's eyes rolled back for a second as he made a dash to attack Phantom. Using every ounce of strength in his GSK moves, he made sure to be methodical in his attack. Just the thought of his team's lives drove him to fight harder. He fought as Phantom laughed at him, blocking and countering every move.

Phantom then grabbed his left arm and pulled him in. He lifted his arm and smashed down on Reaper's, snapping the arm at the elbow. Reaper let out a roar. Then Phantom shouted as he pulled up on Reaper's arm and popped his shoulder out of socket. He used the momentum to twist Reaper and force his head into the wall. Reaper's body dangled for a second through the drywall. He felt a kick to the mid-section that sent him out of the wall and onto his back.

Reaper could feel the pain in his arm and ribs. His already injured arm from their previous encounter now was broken in two places. Blood covered half of his face. He coughed. "Don't…"

Phantom stood over him and raised his hand to check his pulse and rolled his eyes, "Haven't broken a warm up pace yet. But I am impressed. You have heart. Unfortunately you have to know when to lose."

Reaper reached for his hi-cap pistol. Drawing in a fraction of a second, his aim was on. He stared in disbelief as Phantom moved to dodge the weapon and was right on top of him. Phantom grabbed the pistol and turned it into Reaper's chest.

"Remember what I said about guns?" Phantom was face to face with him. "Not like they appear to be helping you out at the moment."

Reaper groaned as he could feel his right hand bending too far. The sound of his wrist twisting the muscles and cartilage made him cringe. The pain in his broken left arm was excruciating as Phantom put more pressure on it.

"Do you really want me to break both?"

"I thought you wanted to kill me?" Reaper grunted.

Phantom eased up and yanked the hi-cap pistol from Reaper's grasp. He tossed it out one of the windows. "I do. I really do. But what is the point in beating you if all you do is die? Not to mention you seem to care a great deal about the others. I can't have you dead without seeing how the rest will turn out." He looked out as if he was watching something outside. "I guess it's time for a reunion with your friends."

"No!" Reaper turned his body to position himself to get up.

"Yes, Reaps, I'm afraid I'll be gone for a moment. But I'll be back to check on you here in a few."

Fear flooded his mind as Reaper struggled to sit up. He fought to his feet but looked up to see Phantom was already gone.

Chapter 21

The area seemed darker, but Violet stayed close. She and Romeo were almost on the floor where he had spotted Provost. Both froze in their place as they heard Reaper shouting. Violet looked at Romeo, "That was Reaper."

Romeo was too focused on his objective, "He'll be fine, let's focus on what we're doing. Besides, if she's here too, we'll have our hands full."

Violet was reluctant to accept his orders, "Fine. But don't kill him," She referred to Provost. She could see it in his eyes, vengeance was on his mind. "Please?"

"We'll see when we get there won't we? If he doesn't try to kill us first." Romeo looked back up the stairs and moved quickly. It was all Violet could do to close the gap and try not to stop him. Then the two made it to the floor where Romeo recalled seeing him. Violet anxiously looked for him to see if she could spot Provost first and get into a better position in case Romeo wanted to simply attack him.

The loud screech in the distance echoed through the hollow floor. Only paneled walls and framed struts scattered throughout the level. Piles of building supplies and materials littered the area. Violet was careful to not make any noise. Since comms were down and their weapons missing, it was obvious that the new team had spotted them first. And more than likely, Provost knew they were coming. She moved slowly along the wall as Romeo treaded in the corners looking for a place to ambush Provost. Her heart was racing. Pandora was lurking in the shadows for sure. It was only a matter of time before she showed her face again.

As they moved deeper into the center of the building, Violet caught a glimpse of a figure. It was her. Violet stayed low and quiet, trying to get Romeo's attention. Using her hands, she signaled for him. After a second, Romeo finally noticed her. She used her hands to signal him that she had spotted Pandora. Romeo looked over to see nothing, but then fast movement caught the corner of his eye. He drew his dagger and followed the direction of the figure. Violet could tell he had spotted her. He pursued his target. Violet hurried to catch up to him. It was going to be difficult to fight someone that could take down Monster on her own. So having at least two of them there may help even the odds. Especially if Provost was setting a trap. She watched as Romeo turned the corner of a wall and stepped forward then froze. Violet turned the corner to assist and noticed what caught his eye.

The man on the chair, was Provost. She observed him further. Then her heart sank. His hands and legs had been restrained to the chair. His face was cut, with the symbols they had seen before. His mouth covered by an adhesive strip.

Violet stepped forward to try and help him. Romeo remained unmoved. Doubt in his eyes. A sudden voice announced its presence in the shadows.

"Ah, Romeo, Romeo. Why thou art?" The man spoke. "I know how and why you're art."

Violet recognized his voice as Dr. Hampton from before. Realizing now he was actually Phantom, the tall operative walked towards them. Separating them from Provost.

"Other Blade members." Phantom continued, "Violet, I presume, his favorite."

The two held their position. Careful not to antagonize the madman before them. And now with the development that Provost was Phantom's prisoner made the situation fragile. Violet thought about how to speak to him. She looked around for Amraam and the others, but they were splitting up and moving slowly through the lower parts of the building. She turned to Romeo, clutching his dagger.

Phantom spoke, "I take it this is more of a surprise for you." He crossed his arms and studied the two. "Why would that be? I thought you wanted him dead?"

Violet's voice cracked, "No, no one needs to die."

He laughed at her, "People always need to die. I know Romeo here realizes that, right? Isn't it Provost that made you live in that hellhole of an Academy? I do recall a report on one fatality, out of 47 students, one died. How ironic it would happen to be your love."

Violet watched Romeo grow agitated.

He continued, "Then after all that, this guy makes you forget about it. He then does his best to make you move past it without any form of apology or acknowledgement for his actions. He has, killing a mere child, on his rap sheet. And now, his old team. "

Violet recalled Provost's orders in the past. Zamora, Camelot; both ex-members of Provost's team.

"Then he made us. Trained us to keep you all in check. Even to kill his last remaining tie, Boss." Phantom projected. "A man like that does not deserve mercy. Isn't that right, Romeo."

Violet became emotional as she saw Provost shake his head. As if he protested. "Don't listen to him, Romeo." She whispered.

"You both need to listen." Phantom told them, "You need to hear it since all you've been doing is running from the truth. Truth is what binds all of us, you see."

Romeo took a step forward but Phantom grinned and threw his hand out. "Uh, just wait. I'll let you have Provost. After all, he owes you that, right?"

Violet could see Romeo stare down Provost. His eyes, piercing with anger.

"But look behind you." Phantom warned.

Violet looked behind her to see Pandora over her shoulder. She instinctively moved to face and swing her hand around in defense. But the woman disappeared. The two looked for her but could find nothing. Then they looked back at Provost, Pandora standing over his shoulder.

Phantom laughed, "See we've been adapted to be far more superior to you, former students of his. Provost made sure we were vastly improved. But then he started to question, again, what he had created. I'll be honest with you. He did want to keep the Cleansing Blade under control, even if it meant to destroy you."

Violet's chest rattled with his words. She could not believe it. Her eyes grew watery as she stared at Provost who looked back at them. Unable to argue back. But based on his reaction, he did not appear to deny what Phantom told them.

Romeo gripped his dagger, it was time to make Provost atone. He stepped towards him but heard Violet calling. "No!" He kept his eyes forward. Violet pleaded, "Romeo, please? He's does not deserve this."

Phantom interrupted, "But he was responsible for the lives of all 47 students. He was responsible for one in particular." He addressed Romeo. "And he wanted to stop the Cleansing Blade, starting with his last tie, Boss. We as his babysitters were to keep tabs on you all. Especially the weakest and most untrustworthy of them all, Romeo." Phantom pointed to him.

Then to Violet, "Violet, he was saving for last. In hopes that she would join his side."

Romeo kept quiet. Violet could not believe Provost just remained still. Only blinking. No moans of denial, or even a nod. Just fear and shame across his face. Violet could not stand the slander from Phantom's mouth. She tried to find something to deter Romeo's rage. "He trained us. He taught us to be better than him. Better than those that harm people on purpose." The words did not seem to faze Romeo. He looked compelled. Violet watched as Romeo lifted his dagger. As if he was going to throw it at Provost. She knew he wanted revenge. He stepped forward again, and lifted his hand that clutched the dagger. The look on his face made Violet fearful that he had lost control of his anger.

Romeo positioned the knife to be thrown. He took another step and swung his arm out, tossing the knife. Violet watched as he released it further to the right and straight towards Phantom. She felt slight relief until she witnessed Phantom turn his body and snag the knife as it passed by him. He held the knife in his hand while Romeo stood in disbelief.

Phantom shook his head. "Ah, the dagger of Romeo." He observed the blade, "Live? No 'die' on the other side?"

The two Cleansing Blade operatives stood still.

Phantom laughed, "Because if you live by the blade, then you shall die by the blade." He swung his hand and threw the blade at Provost. But in the split second, Pandora crouched and grabbed the blade. Stopping it just a fingernail's width from Provost's chest.

Violet stepped forward, fearing the worst. She knew they would not hesitate, but curiosity intruded her thoughts. They were playing games with them. Perhaps in hopes to gain their allegiance. Or it was to break them slowly. Provost's face shocked her. She was witnessing her mentor, her teacher carry fear across his face.

Phantom backed away from them keeping his arm out. "All good and bad people must come to an end." He dropped his hand and disappeared backwards into the shadows.

Violet looked on in disbelief as Pandora thrust the knife into Provost's chest. She forced Provost on his back as the chair fell. Violet and Romeo dashed over but Pandora was too quick and disappeared in the darkness of the floor. "God, please no." Violet prayed as she knelt over Provost who struggled to breathe. She removed his tape so that he could speak. "It's okay. We're here, now." Violet said. She studied the wound. Knowing full well he was doomed, she knew not to remove the blade since it would cause massive bleeding and he would die that much faster.

"They must," He struggled to speak, "Stopped."

Violet saw Romeo stand over them. "Let's worry about you first." A flood of Phantom's words filled her mind. She tried to fight it but could not resist, "Is it true what Phantom said? Did you really want us dead? What about Boss? Did you have him killed?"

Provost's gray eyes were watery. He tried at shaking his head in objection. "No." His voice was starting to fade. "I made them, yes. But..." His breathing slowed. "in case you...lost your way." Violet grabbed his hand and she felt him clutch it. "I regret..." She fought back the tears. He turned to look over at Romeo, struggling to keep conscious. "everything...." He whispered as he started to drift. "I'm ....s..." Violet felt his hand loosen its grip as he let out his last sigh. His eyes fell back with his head.

"I'm calling it." Violet whispered. "He's gone." She remained composed. Her hand gently moved to shut his eyes and continued down his face and to his chest where it stopped on Romeo's dagger. She wrapped her fingers around the handle then tightened her grip and pulled the blade from the lifeless body. She stood up and held the blade in front of Romeo. Blood dripping down the end of the blade.

"I know this isn't what you truly wanted." She spoke straight forward. "But I hope this is enough blood for you." She tossed the blade to the floor and proceeded out of the room.

Romeo looked down at the blade. He could not believe what he had witnessed. He bent down to pick the dagger off the floor. Holding it tightly, he watched the red blood drip down to the handle. His mind filled with thoughts of the Academy. He found himself back at the campus grounds. He gave a death stare at the blade. On the ground near the old dorms, Julia's body lay lifeless. The same dagger. The feeling was the same. Pure dread and regret filled him. The night Julia died because of him. And now, Provost. He felt worthless, guilty. Not one ounce of relief found its way to him. Phantom was right, it needed to have 'die' on it. Since that's all it was good for. He thought of Provost's last words; regret. Romeo closed his eyes for a second. The mission grew dire. This new team was far more effective and dangerous than he had perceived. Romeo could feel the odds stacking against them.

Chapter 22

Reaper struggled to sit up against the broken wall. He could feel his arm dangle from his shoulder. It needed to be reset. He reached around with his good hand and grabbed his shoulder. His eyes rolled back and he gave it a yank. Careful not to make too much noise, he endured the pain that seared through his body. He heard the click and tried moving his shoulder. It seemed to lodge back into place. It would still need to be reset and worked on properly; that is, if he survived. Next he could see that his elbow was bent in the opposite direction. It was time to try and reset it, too. Using some of the basic medical training and taking notes from Violet, he assessed the elbow with his fingers. Violet was nowhere near him to help assess his own injuries. Feeling around the snapped arm and wishing for a real medic; it was a mission of dire straits, and self-preservation came with the territory in the field. He needed to get back with the others. No telling what Romeo and Violet were after, and Phantom proved to be better in every way imaginable. It was going to take all of them to stop Provost and his new team.

With a few more gentle squeezes, the elbow appeared only to be knocked out of its socket. Perhaps a small fracture above it. Either way, it needed to be reset but this one was much worse. Reaper reached into the satchel of his vest, and grabbed a small syringe of the Adrenaline Solution booster. It helped to speed up the healing process as well as took care of pain with little effect on the mind. He pulled the lid off with his mouth and drove the needle into his arm. The burning was minimal and he could immediately feel its effects. Now it was time to pull himself back together and find the others. He struggled to his feet and found a stack of wooden 2 by 4's near the constructed office. One would become a brace. He bent to pull the board out and turned around to sit. He positioned the board between himself and his arm. Feeling his bicep flat against the piece of wood, Reaper rolled his eyes back to brace for the pain. Remembering to relax his arm, he grabbed onto his forearm and yanked it forward. The clicking noise came with a huge amount of pain causing his muscles to tremble.

Reaper took a breath to compose himself. He observed his arm looking normal again. The board did its job as he stood up slowly. He turned back and felt his arm hanging. He tightened his left hand to make sure there was no nerve damage. All felt fine but his elbow. The pain was excruciating as he managed to lift it up. It was going to have to do.

The silence of the floor he was on was soon interrupted by footsteps. He counted one set. He recalled Phantom not making any noise while he stepped. It was more than likely his own team. The steps were fast, careless yet cautious. Once she turned the corner, Reaper felt relief.

"Thank God." Gothica holstered her crossbow pistol. "I was afraid of what I would find. What the hell were you thinking?"

He could tell she was disappointed in him, "Team's safety."

"And yours?" She knelt down to him.

Reaper looked at her as she bent down to help him. "I didn't think he really was that good." He fought hard not to tell her the real reason was her safety and feeling the chances of having a normal life slowly fading. He shook out of it, "Thank you, Gothica."

"I'm sorry, what was that?" She was snide.

"Gothica." Reaper grinned. He caught himself.

"That's what I thought. No names." She shook her head. "Those bind us back to the normal world, remember? Lives we left behind."

He sensed she missed her old life. Her saying that made him recall his own name then Aurora's, Catherine. He tried to fight the memories of the last time he used that name. She had died shortly after he called her that. His stomach curdled with the thought of calling Gothica by her real name. His thought was broken up by the sound of two sets of footsteps. Gothica greeted the two as they entered. He was happy to see Radical and Motherboard still okay.

"Need help?" Radical moved to him.

Reaper's voice was raspy, "How'd you know I need assistance?"

Radical grinned, "Strange really, almost like a little voice telling us you were in trouble."

Motherboard chimed in, "And not to mention, seeing your signature on the Cat-Eye flying around made it easy to figure out."

They moved to help him stand. Radical checked him. "You injured bad?"

"Just my arm. He broke it, twice."

Radical felt his arm. "Where?"

"Shoulder and elbow. Knocked them out of socket." he grumbled.

Radical looked over at Gothica, noticing her body sustained no injuries. "How come you're not injured?"

"Because, Reaper," Gothica looked at him. "Saved me."

"Good work." Radical shrugged at Reaper. "Need to reset your arm?" He asked.

"No, just finished doing that."

Motherboard looked at him, "Need a booster?"

"Took care of it." Reaper smiled.

"This is like déjà vu." Radical chuckled. "Only backwards and we're not on a ship."

Reaper smiled, "Good thing you're observant then. What about the others?"

Radical shook his head. "You're probably not going to like this. But when we met up with Amraam in the central lobby, Oracle was not with him."

"What?"

Motherboard elaborated with him, "Also, her signature disappeared off our sensors. We can't find her with this 'fancy gadget' nor with comms."

"Oooh." Radical commented, "That was low. Poor guy's paralyzed and you're still throwing blows at him?"

"No, just saying. How she could've disappeared doesn't make sense. And I don't want to assume anything, but." Motherboard implied Oracle's defection. She could have returned to Provost's new team. Romeo's theory of her being the third made Reaper worry.

Reaper felt defeated. Oracle was the first woman in years that he had fallen for. And the first woman whom he'd ever felt passion with. If she had betrayed them, would he have to fight her too? He shook out of it, "You're right, no assumptions. But we know that Phantom is here, as well as Violet and Romeo finding someone else." He noticed Radical still had his pistol strapped to his leg, "And those, we don't need them. They led us here because they knew the police would be here with the first sound of gunfire they heard. And then, who knows what they'll do."

"Sounds like we need a solution." Radical said, "And really any major problem can be solved with the use of high explosives."

"Oh great, not this speech again." Motherboard pulled out her flex pad. Her quick fingers began to type away.

Radical smiled wide, "Got a better idea?"

Reaper looked over at Motherboard, "What are you doing?"

"I haven't had time to search for the signal they're using to block our comms." Motherboard swiped away. "I see it."

"And?" Radical teased.

"It looks like our own. Same frequency is blocking itself. But..." She continued.

"But?" Radical persisted.

"The signal is blocking itself. Using a small wave in synch with our own." She looked closely. The screen was lit up and reflected off of her glasses.

Radical noticed the reflection. "Looks complicated."

"Got it." Motherboard grew excited. "I found and isolated the signal. But the source seems to move. And there are two sources."

"Meaning?" Reaper held his arm.

"Meaning," Motherboard looked at them, "The two agents we're after are the source of the signals."

"Anyway to stop it?"

"I can counter it." Motherboard continued, "But I can't erase it. If I do counter though, that means their comms and ours may be all on one channel."

Reaper thought for a second. It was overwhelming, Oracle, Phantom, and now sharing a comms with the enemy. Was it worth the risk? Reluctantly, Reaper turned over to Radical. "I don't want to say it. But do you have any ideas?"

Radical's eyes lit up. "As a matter of fact, I do. Since they appear to be good at traps, I think we should set up one of our own."

"How?"

"Simple. We get their attention and then, make a run for it to the area that I rig up. Then boom." He laughed.

"Boom?" Gothica interrupted, "Really?

Reaper turned back to Motherboard, "So what's your plan?"

Motherboard looked at him. "Actually, I'm about to implement it now."

Gothica shook her head, "Is it better than blowing up this building?"

Radical defended, "Hey. If you listen closely that loud noise coming from down the road is coming from more development in the area. If I sync it with that noise, no one would know."

"Except all of the broken glass on that apartment complex." Motherboard was good at killing his plans.

"So then what are you doing?" Reaper asked her.

"If I figured out that there are two signal sources, then I can calibrate the Cat-Eye and our sensors to pinpoint the exact location of the two sources. Thus, pinpointing the exact locations of where our two friends are."

Radical moved over to give her a pat on the shoulder, "Wow, that's pretty awesome."

Motherboard shrugged off his gesture. "I know. Plus it saves poor billionaire, Alan Frey, his building."

Reaper was pleased, "Excellent work Motherboard, as usual." He thought about the threat they faced; if Phantom could take him on and so easily out match him, the entire team could still be at a disadvantage. And as his role as leader, all the prospects and options to accomplish the mission needed to be looked at closely. "But I hate to say this." He bit his lower lip. "We may need a contingency plan if we can't beat them once we find them. So Radical."

"Yes sir." He said with great enthusiasm.

"Figure out a way to make the blast lethal enough without causing this building to collapse." Reaper ordered.

Gothica warned, "New Yorkers are pretty sour about that kind of thing."

"You got it," Radical reached into his satchel to look at all of his explosive tools and options. "I'll keep it low profile. These cannon bombs have proven to be helpful before, with just enough to make whoever is close enough sorry."

"Try not to enjoy it too much either, jeez." Gothica looked sort of frightened by him.

"Good." Reaper looked around the room. He used his Cat-Eye to scan for the other members of the team. It was clear Violet and Romeo were fixed on one floor. Violet knelt. Was she injured? Then just one more figure on the lower level of the building, Amraam. No sign of Oracle. He shook his head. Could she have fooled them? Him? It was a lot to take in, but for now, the mission needed to carry on.

Gothica looked at him, "So then, what are we doing?"

Reaper looked at them. He knew it was too hard to try and accomplish this on his own. Even if it was for the sake of his team. He took a deep breath to concentrate, recalling Phantom's last words to him, "I have an idea." He looked at Gothica, "But you're not going to like it. Being that Oracle is MIA, we have to be extra cautious. Whether she defected back to them or they killed her," He paused to absorb his own words. The idea hurt him but he tried to stay on track. "That means we need to stay focused. Phantom told me he's coming back for me. In which case, Radical, I need you to booby trap this area, where I'll wait for him, alone."

"No," Gothica fought his decision, "You don't get it. He'll kill you this time."

"That's fine." Reaper did not know how else to respond. "I'm tired of running from them. We face them here tonight. And if we die trying, then so be it."

Radical spoke up, looking around, "Wow, I didn't think you would ever say that. But I like your thinking. And I'll get to work here."

Gothica remained unmoved, "Listen, it will take all of us…"

"Exactly." Reaper argued back, "And if Pandora and Provost are here, and Oracle," he gritted, "Then we need to focus on them, and take advantage of Phantom being alone with me."

She seemed disappointed, but then she knew what he was doing, "I appreciate what you're trying to do. But let me help you here."

"No." Reaper was sturdy, "Your orders are to find and eliminate the threats. I will handle Phantom. Radical," He nodded to him. "Motherboard? Initiate your program to locate them. Then meet with the others and converge on our enemies."

Radical began to work on the room with his explosives. Motherboard proceeded to leave the room, "Once I initiate, it will take a few minutes to solidify their signals, good luck."

Gothica approached Reaper and gave him a cruel stare, "These orders are ridiculous. And I strongly object."

Reaper grinned at her, "I'm adapting. And if we make it through this, then you'll know I have my reasons."

Gothica shook her head, "I'll try and trust your judgement then. And I won't question it again, if we survive." With that she took off and left him. He looked over at Radical who was placing his last explosive.

Radical approached him, "These cannon bombs are designed to explode in a certain direction. Minimizing collateral damage, of course. If you can help it, get him somewhere in this area." Radical pointed out the area near the extra building material and near the wall. "Now these charges are in sync with your wrist pad. There are two settings, instant boom and timed boom." He instructed, "Red means instant. Orange means timed which triggers a twenty second countdown."

"Are you sure these will work?" Reaper questioned the explosives expert.

Radical smiled, "I am certain. They will work."

"Gotchya." Reaper acknowledged.

"Good luck." With that, Radical left to join the others.

"You too." Reaper acknowledged. He studied the area. Radical had placed three bombs all at key points that would engulf the space he was in. He looked around. It was time to sit tight, hope the team would make it, and wait for Phantom.

Section 5:

The Box

Chapter 23

Amraam searched the next floor. As to how Oracle could have vanished without a trace made him more cautious. His trusty P90 submachinegun in hand, he proceeded to check the next floor, making his way up to meet Violet and Romeo halfway back down. He checked his corners, remembering his training. It was important to sweep at an angle. Though he figured with an enemy with common training, it was going to be a matter of who spotted who first. He turned to check his six. He noticed three signals were approaching him soon. Then he looked up to see another signal high in the north tower. His mind raced wondering who had stayed behind, or who they left for dead.

He turned back to see Violet's signature getting closer. She appeared to be on the same level. Sections of the walls were in place. Making a maze of sorts throughout the 15th floor. He proceeded to meet up with Violet. As she turned the corner to see him, he was taken back by the look on her face. She did not appear to look like the sweet girl he knew; she seemed serious, almost resentful. "Is everything okay?"

She looked up at him, "No. We have a problem."

Amraam held his gun tightly, "What kind of problem?"

"Provost is dead." Violet's voice was toneless.

"He's what?" Amraam was in shock, "Tell me you didn't…"

Violet's green eyes met with his, "No. His new agents have gone rogue. They killed him."

"Oh boy." he thought about what they had just seen.

Violet's soft voice showed little emotion, but desperation was still clear on her face. "We need to stop them."

Amraam could see she was holding up and nodded, "Well, what are we waiting for." He noticed Romeo clear the corner. He appeared stricken. "What's your status?"

Romeo was silent.

"He's alive." Violet spoke for him. "They killed Provost in front of us." Her tone was shifting. She became angry.

Amraam remained calm, "Look, we're here now. We know the targets are here, two, possibly three."

"Three?" Violet asked.

"Yeah," Amraam whispered, "I lost Oracle. Not sure how or even where she went."

Violet searched the area, "Then if we have to deal with her too, we will."

Amraam studied them. They both appeared to be missing their sidearms. "What happen to your weapons?"

"Pandora disarmed us." Violet said. "Right from under our noses."

Violet seemed conflicted to feel no remorse. It was almost frightening to see her this way. Amraam tried to think of something reassuring to tell her. His nerves were unsteady. "Hey," He approached her, "If our mission is to stop them, then that's what we're going to do. They will pay for what they did to Boss, and Provost." His look of confidence seemed contagious as Violet seemed to crack a smile. He looked over at the silent Romeo, "Are you gonna be okay?"

Romeo stood still, as if he was lost. "Ask me when this is over."

Amraam could feel the morale begin to decline. Then his Cat-Eye seemed to glitch and restart. He looked around, the sensors from his teammates were good. Then he noticed another signature moving strangely around the same floor. He turned around as he heard more footsteps. Gothica and the others approached him. "Glad you made it." He counted them, "Where's Reaper?"

Gothica sounded irritated. "He stayed behind. Figured taking on Phantom alone again would help us out." Her tone was condescending.

Motherboard spoke up, "I've calibrated the lens now to show us where the two may be hiding."

Amraam looked around, the foreign signal flashed around the floor, moving abnormally fast. "At least we can see them moving. How'd you do that?"

"It's technical." Motherboard responded, fixing her glasses. "And now's not the time."

Amraam looked around, only the one was close. He raised his P90.

"I'd watch that." Gothica warned. "Any gunfire may alert the authorities. And if that happens, the stakes will be that much greater."

Her point was valid, but not having a warm gun in his hands was not his standard operating procedure. "Let's spread out then. One is right on top of us."

The team was in alert mode. Each spread out, watching the signature of one of their enemies move from side to side. It seemed to be navigating the floor to get closer to them. Amraam saw Violet move to the far wall. Romeo remained still, his dagger in hand. It appeared to have fresh blood stains on it. It was clear now. The dagger must have been used to kill Provost. He did not even want to think about how. Then out of the corner of his eye, he caught movement. The figure grabbed Violet and threw her to the ground, then vanished. The tracker on his Cat-Eye followed the signal. It was moving fast and around them.

He turned to see Radical at the ready. But before he could react, the figure moved to him and struck him in the face. Amraam did not recognize her. It must have been Pandora. She twisted Radical's hand and forced him to the ground. Before Amraam had a chance to react, she disappeared again. She moved with finesse and precision. As if she had practiced evading in a hurry, for a century. Romeo passed him on the pursuit. Amraam turned to go help Violet up. "Are you okay?"

She coughed. "Yeah, got the jump on me." A loud shout came from the other side of the wall.

"Motherboard." Amraam and Violet moved to aide their teammate. As they turned the corner, they stumbled into a dead end. "This place is a labyrinth." They doubled back and noticed Radical run towards the sound. The signals showed Pandora and Motherboard separated from the rest. It seemed like Gothica was the closest. Romeo next to her. Amraam analyzed their placement. "She's separating us. Gonna try to take on and kill us one at a time."

Violet sounded determined, "Not tonight."

Amraam was thrown off. Seeing Violet like this made him feel strangely at ease. Her vulnerability made him fight harder, however; now with her in a fearless mode, made her seem to be fighting harder than him. The way things appeared at the moment, they were all going to need to be in fighting shape to take on this challenge.

They spotted Gothica looking down at what appeared to be a narrow hallway as if she had located them, crossbow in hand. Romeo was on the opposite side of the wall. Amraam watched Radical move past Gothica, who was holding her position.

"Drop the girl." Gothica ordered.

"Let her go." Radical warned. "Or things are going to get really bad for you real quick."

Pandora held Motherboard close to her, a small blade in hand. Motherboard was calm. A slice marked her cheek. She stood still as Pandora controlled their backward movements. Moon and city light from the outside poured in from the window behind them. Pandora looked steady. The look on her face never shifted, it remained focused.

"Motherboard, just stay calm." Radical assured. "No need to get excited."

"You should listen to yourself more often." Motherboard was still snarky.

Pandora raised her small knife to Motherboard's throat.

"She's gonna kill her." Radical shouted.

Amraam looked down the hall to see Romeo in position. He was going to make his move. Amraam drew his P90. The situation was grim and it was time to save Motherboard.

Chapter 24

Reaper noticed the signal getting closer, moving smoothly up the building. It was a different color than his team's. He knew it was Phantom. Reaper looked around at the explosive points that Radical had set. Well hidden, it was only a matter of getting Phantom in the same room, and himself out. He figured the best way to convince Phantom he was still injured, was to pretend he was barely recuperating from their previous encounter. It was only a matter of time. He thought about the others as his scanner picked up on them moving around the same floor with the second enemy signal. The team was on the offensive. But would they be able to handle Pandora? He knelt down. Recalling Aurora's advice, along with Gothica's, it was time to believe in his team. And right now, it was time to believe in himself. The corner of his eye caught a glimpse of a face. "Now Reaps, do you really think I'm a fool?" the voice chuckled. Reaper turned to face him, but he was gone. It was Phantom. The tracker showed him moving quickly down the hall and back through the hole he had made using Reaper's body earlier.

"You really think I don't know that your friends came here?" Phantom stood in front of him.

Reaper stood up. He held his arm back and remained silent. Assessing his foe and how it was possible to stop him one on one.

"I figured they have enough on their plate already." Phantom continued, "As for you, I told you I would come back. And I am a man of my word."

"I knew you were." Reaper spoke, showing no fear.

"I assume you're ready for me then. Perhaps have something up your sleeve, yes?"

Reaper grinned, "I might."

"Cat and mouse not fun anymore, huh?" Phantom smiled, "Well then, I guess lambs to the wolf."

"Why did you let them live?" Reaper thought about his team.

"Simply because what they know, and what they don't. Like I said, they will have enough on their plate once they meet Pandora. Then once I'm done here, I'll kill the rest if she left any."

"You sound pretty sure of that."

"Oh I am." Phantom lifted his hands. "You see, Reaps." He displayed himself. "If you think I'm scary. You haven't seen anything yet."

Reaper felt uneasy. "So if Pandora can handle them. Is Provost gonna just sit and watch?"

Phantom glared at him. "You must not know. Ah that's right. I blocked your communications. Provost is disposed of."

"What?" Reaper felt weak in the knees.

"Yes. I'm afraid his services were no longer required. Thanks to Romeo, that is."

Reaper felt jostled. He knew Romeo was hell-bent on revenge, but he thought he knew him better than that. He struggled to believe it. "You're wrong. Even he wouldn't just kill him."

Phantom's laugh filled the empty room. "Are you sure?"

"I know my team."

"I suppose you do. Well, I mean, thanks to his dagger. He made Pandora's hand slip and kill the old man."

Reaper felt weak. Phantom had killed Provost. "Why are you doing this?"

"The famous question that all must account for." Phantom smiled, "Why? Why are you doing this, Reaps?"

"Because there is a greater good. And I'll stand by that. Even if it means stopping you." Reaper breathed heavily.

"Is that really the case, Reaps?" Phantom interrogated, "Is that really why you do this? Because you're good? What defines good is simply what we believe. Purely subjective."

"You're wrong."

"Oh? How so?"

Reaper stood up straight. "Believing in something that is good, means you will sacrifice yourself and your own wellbeing for others. Pure logic. Even deep down, Provost believed that."

"Yes, and now he's dead. Though his original goal was to keep you in check. And terminate the Cleansing Blade, if necessary."

Reaper looked back down to see Pandora's signal close to what appeared to be Motherboard's. As if she had her. He remained composed for the moment. "If that's the case why follow through? If Provost is dead, then why come after us still? If anything, you and I, we're the same now. Our teams are the same."

Phantom grinned, "You got that part right. We are the same, Reaps. In more ways than you might know."

Reaper grew confused. "What do you mean?"

"Both sides are the spawn of Provost's fancy experiments." He explained, "Remnants of part of a Solution."

Reaper was confused, "Solution? The Enhancer?"

"Yes. Three of us, volunteers." Phantom explained, "Enlightened by Provost's generous offer, we took the oath to join his ranks. He wanted fresh bodies to test something he had been working on. Something in regards to genetics."

"What did he need you for when he had us?" Reaper questioned Provost's actions more. "We adapted to the Adrenaline Solution. Why not continue it on us?"

Phantom's eyes widened with excitement. "Simply put, Reaps, he grew afraid of you and needed to test it on someone new. After two years of transformation. You, who adapted to the

Adrenaline Solution, were then used to enhance a new solution."

Reaper tried piecing the clues together. "Us?"

"Yes. The Cleansing Blade's members all adapted superbly to the Adrenaline Solution. Their genes, in turn, could handle it. With that, Provost used your genetic variants to create something more. Genetically altering us volunteers to adapt better. You see with my adapting, plus yours, you get the Enhancer Solution."

"He used us to make you?"

Phantom appeared to be enjoying it, "Yes, your genetic codes were infused with our own and created beings far more superior to you."

The words rattled him.

"To put it simply, Reaps. We were genetically altered by the Cleansing Blade members. You plus old me, equals new me."

He studied the man before him. It made sense. Much to Reaper's dismay. He recalled his story, "You said three volunteers? Oracle?"

Phantom nodded, "Yes I did. And you mean blind woman? Don't be silly, Reaps. She's unfit for our caliber. The third died due to the Enhancer Solution deforming his body and eating it from the inside. Provost had it disposed of somewhere unknown. The process even costed Pandora her vocal cords."

The words brought a glimmer of hope to Reaper. Maybe Oracle was good. But if that was case, where did she go? And did they kill her first?

"After the transition, Provost had trained us. Fortified what we had already known and with the Enhancer, made us more. It allowed us to take full control of our bodies. Simply to turn any pain or feeling, off completely." Phantom grinned. "Full mental control of our own bodies."

"If Provost wanted something more, then why target us? We gave him no reason to fear us."

"Because, since we adapted so well, Provost insisted we remain as guardians for him and his precious Cleansing Blade. We did for a while and kept you under a close watch. Then it became clear to me." Phantom's voice dropped, "Men like him don't change. It would've been a matter of time before he created something to control us."

"I take it that being replaced would hurt your feelings?" Reaper toyed back.

Phantom's face held a smile, "I grew tired to just watching. I wanted a challenge, and I wanted to test the Cleansing Blade."

Reaper knew what was coming as Phantom stepped forward. "So how'd we do?"

"Well, I'm a little disappointed." Phantom crossed his arms, "If you can't challenge us, or be able to stop us, then I'll just have to start a war."

Reaper believed every word; Phantom could not be stopped if he and the Cleansing Blade failed. Provost was dead, the realization that this team had no bounds. If Phantom and

Pandora succeeded in their mission, the world would be at stake. "So then what are you waiting for?" Reaper had his one chance, he pressed the bomb timer on his wrist pad; twenty seconds. "Kill me then!"

Reaper braced for Phantom's charge. His mind was foggy and the pain in his arm affected it. As he felt Phantom's hands striking against his torso, the pain from his injuries clouded his concentration. Suddenly it stopped and his mind was clear and focused. Reaper did not have time to think as to why it was. But he found himself blocking Phantom's strikes. Reaper could focus on his opponent. He then turned to the offensive. He made GSK strikes at Phantom but every move was blocked. Phantom grabbed him by his injured arm and hoisted him to the pile of wooden 2 by 4's.

His body crashed over them. Reaper rolled back and stood behind them. He grabbed one and prepared to use it as a weapon. Before he could make his move, Phantom grabbed the piece of wood and twisted it out of Reaper's grasp and struck Reaper in the head with it.

"No weapons, Reaps." Phantom threw the piece of wood against the wall.

Reaper tried to regain composure. He looked down at his wrist pad, the red light blinking ten seconds. He shook it off and stood up. Raising his hands for combat he could feel his adrenaline spike as the countdown got closer to zero. "Phantom!"

"Reaper!" Phantom shouted. "It is time!"

Reaper charged at his foe. He knew it was time, death was near. With his strikes, his fist finally found Phantom's face. But Phantom turned back and smiled. He grabbed Reaper's arm and twisted it to leave him vulnerable. On his way down he slammed Reaper's head against the stack of wood and pulled him up. Reaper countered the next punch to his face by tilting his head. It would've been lights out for sure. He felt Phantom then pull him back and sent a front kick to his midsection. Reaper felt the impact of his back smash through the wall behind him.

"This is getting ridiculous, Reaps." Phantom sounded angry. "You can take a beating, I'll give you that. And I'm waiting for your next move."

Reaper looked back at his wrist pad.

2…

1…

The wall disintegrated before him as he felt the concussion. In the haze, he felt his mind drifting. Once again he found himself on the hillside of a mountain. The night sky was filled with an aurora borealis. He had been there before. Then her voice resonated through the hills. "Not yet. You don't get to die here." Aurora's words to him long ago. Reaper quickly shot out of the dream. His ears were ringing. He could see dust and smoke around him. Rubble buried him partially. He struggled to stand. The wall he had been cast through was no longer there. The blast had removed it along with the back wall of the large office room.

Reaper felt pain in his chest as he took a breath. The dust made him cough. Excruciating pain shot from his midsection. Broken ribs for sure. He spit up blood on the floor. He could feel his eyes watering and burning as he tried sitting up. The blast had caused his sinuses to rupture, again causing blood to slowly leak from his tear duct. He tried to remain composed. Then as the dust cleared he saw the figure standing just a few feet away, facing him. Phantom appeared unfazed by the blast. Reaper's heart sank. He knew Phantom was going to kill him. Reaper knew that his body could not physically handle another close encounter with him. This time, he would allow the Dark Phantom to take him.

Reaper struggled to stand but could not. He made it to his knees, knowing the end was coming. Phantom approached him slowly. He could see Phantom had little blood on his face from the blast. It did not appear to affect him at all. Reaper took a breath. Fighting through the pain to enjoy the air flow through his nose one last time. Phantom then stood over him. Reaper slowly lifted his head to see him eye to eye.

Phantom shook his head. "If you can't beat them, then destroy everything around them? Come on, Reaps, only to fail and die on your knees?"

Reaper could hear something in his voice. Like he needed to clear it. He assessed his foe. Appearing strong and unstoppable, except… Reaper's eyes widened. It looked as if a piece of wood was sticking out of Phantom's neck. He found what little strength he could to stand. He met eyes with his adversary as he stood straight up.

"That's better." Phantom grinned.

"You said you cannot feel pain?" Reaper struggled to speak. "Then you cannot feel life either."

Phantom smiled wide, "Getting all emotional are we?" He reached to wipe the bloody tear streaks from Reaper's face. "I feel what I want to feel. That's what I trained to perfect."

Reaper gazed at him. "Then, I guess you'll never feel death coming."

"I see death," He stepped face to face with Reaper, "And laugh." Phantom drove his hands into Reaper's neck, carrying him across the hallway and slammed him up against the next wall. "Now do YOU feel death coming?"

Reaper could no longer breathe. He placed his hands upon Phantom's tight grip around his neck. He started to lose consciousness but saw the piece of wood still lodged in Phantom's neck. He moved his hands to cup Phantom's neck and was met with a smile as Phantom mocked the attempt to choke him back. But Reaper made his move. He grabbed the shard and yanked it out. Reaper's eyes widened as he lifted the piece in front of Phantom's face. Phantom looked at it. Noticing the blood. He looked down and saw the blood stream go down his arm and fall from his elbow to the floor. Phantom released Reaper and stepped back.

Reaper immediately fell to the floor, gasping for air. He looked up to see Phantom standing above him with a smile.

"So," Phantom's voice cracked as he gargled on his own blood. "That's what you meant."

Reaper was shocked that Phantom seemed unfazed.

"What will my love say?" Phantom looked around.

Reaper listened to his words.

"Pandora!" Phantom called to her as he dropped to one knee. He looked back at Reaper and smiled, giving him chills. "I feel sorry for you all."

All Reaper could do was look at him. Then Phantom began to laugh. Reaper stared as the man laughed in his face. Blood pouring out of his neck and now his mouth. Then he collapsed slowly to the floor, still laughing. Reaper crawled and pulled himself up to kneel next the dying man. He noticed the laughter ceasing and Phantom slowly dying. Then silence. Reaper looked at his foe, motionless, then the body jolted and sprawled out, causing Reaper to fall back. What he witnessed was the body start to burn itself. He recalled Aurora, knowing that this is what had happened to her, too. But this time, the Enhancer Solution must have come with a quicker effect of spontaneous combustion. Reaper watched as Phantom's body quickly burned to a dark ash. He let out a breath and turned around, using his lens to track the others. He recalled the words of Phantom, warning him about Pandora. She was going to kill them all.

Chapter 25

Violet stood back and watched as Pandora held her comrade tightly. The hallway stretched back to a window overlooking the street below. After all they had experienced, Violet remained composed. Motherboard did not appear to be worried, either. But that was subject to change. Violet flinched as she heard a loud boom coming from the north tower. Fearing the worst she looked at Radical who approached Pandora with a smile.

"You hear that?" Radical asked the quiet woman. "That's the sound of the other one of you blowing up." He threw up his hands, "Boom. Dead."

"Are you trying to help me," Motherboard mumbled, "Or piss her off?"

Pandora seemed unfazed. Like his words were nothing more than a bluff. Then she looked as if she was checking her wrist. Violet noticed it looked like a small screen. Possibly a mission pad that was small like a watch. Violet saw it in her face. Pandora looked like she knew something. Something bad. Violet looked over to see Romeo's signal on the other side of the wall where he waited to bust through and ambush her. She turned back to see Pandora. Her face showed what could be sadness, then pure resentment, then back to mellow. She did not appear to acknowledge much from what she saw, but Violet could see something in her eyes and it made her skin crawl.

Suddenly, the wall exploded with Romeo ready to attack. Pandora stepped back with Motherboard held close, and grabbed his hand with the dagger. Motherboard struck Pandora's hand, knocking the small knife from her grasp. Pandora pulled Romeo's dagger hand in and used it to slice Motherboard across the face. Pandora released her and kicked her through the hole in the wall. She pulled Romeo in and racked his arm backwards as his body moved forward, his blade still in his hand. Radical jumped to help him but Pandora pulled Romeo and twisted him till he flipped. She then prepared for Radical and grabbed him. She drove her knee into his stomach, lifting him from the ground. Using the momentum, she slammed him through the wall. Violet approached but Gothica cut in between and prepared to attack.

She tucked and fired a bolt from her crossbow. Pandora moved to dodge it and snagged it from the air as she spun around. Gothica made an attempt to attack but Pandora was right on top of her. Pandora grabbed her wrist and drove the bolt through her arm. She torqued the bolt forcing Gothica to move to the wall. Pandora noticed Romeo behind her as he moved to drive his dagger into her, but she was too fast. She sidestepped, avoiding Romeo, and moved to grab his dagger. Ramming her elbow into his face, she ripped it from his grasp as she drove her boot into his leg. The leg he had injured on a prior mission. Pandora then turned her body, Gothica's arm in hand and Romeo's dagger in the other. She swiped at Romeo, slicing his ear as he tried to dodge her attack. Gothica's moans of pain were only met with Pandora driving the dagger into her stomach as Romeo tried to knock Pandora off balance. She kicked Romeo to the floor with a thunderous thump.

"No!" Violet shouted. She charged forward, watching as Gothica fell to the floor. Pandora placed her boot on top of Gothica's sternum and pulled the dagger out of her stomach. She stepped aside as Violet attacked. Pandora swiped up with the knife. Violet managed to avoid it. Pandora grabbed her and used her as a shield just as Amraam drew his weapon.

He yielded as she held Violet close. But before he could think of his next move, Violet attempted to throw her. She broke free and Pandora swiped the blade at her, narrowly missing her neck and instead severing her braid. Pandora kicked Violet forwards and threw the blade towards Violet's back. Amraam dashed as the blade careened towards her. He braced as the blade lodged into his shoulder before Violet's braid hit the floor. Amraam flinched from the impact, he looked back to see Pandora in front of him. She grabbed his P90. As he tried to out muscle her, Amraam was thrown off balance. Pandora had twisted his wrist. She jabbed her hand into blade handle, smashing it deeper into his shoulder, causing him to react to the pain. He felt it go through to his back. She spun around him and lifted his arm till it popped out of socket. Ripping the gun from his grasp, Pandora kicked out his knee to drop him and smashed him in the head with the butt of his gun.

Violet stood up on her knees after witnessing Amraam's sacrifice. She caught sight of Pandora as she threw the gun at her. Violet barely managed to avoid it. She saw Romeo and Radical behind Pandora. Gothica, holding onto her stomach, had managed to have an arrow in her crossbow. Motherboard was moving, avoiding the chaos. She seemed to be bleeding from her face, but still working on her mission pad. Amraam forced himself off the floor, enduring the pain.

Pandora stood in the middle of them. For a second nobody moved, Violet then charged in, stepping onto her braid before she met face to face with their enemy. Violet moved to strike her but Pandora dodged and grabbed her hand. She rotated her arm and slammed down on Violet's arm and shoved her aside to anticipate Radical. Pandora twisted her body around his as he swung towards her. She wrapped her arm around his neck and pulled him over end. Slamming him to the ground. Radical tried to recover quickly but was met with a stomp to the head and kicked back against the broken wall. Romeo dashed for Pandora. Violet knew he was adamant about his training in GSK. If anyone could match her speed, it was him.

Romeo took a breath and moved to the offensive but Pandora blocked his moves and smashed her hand against his cut ear. Romeo fought to ignore the pain and tried to throw her. With all of his might he grabbed her and attempted to slam her to the floor. He knew he was over powering her but she twisted her body and slipped out of his grip. She drove a kick back into his leg. He knew better than to show pain, but it was too much. He quivered for a second. Enough to give Pandora the leverage she needed to escape. Romeo tried to avoid another attack from her. He saw Pandora dodge another arrow from Gothica's crossbow and Pandora turned around and grabbed it midair. Romeo tried to avoid her as she slammed the arrow into his shoulder. Just an inch from his neck. She dropped Romeo to his knees and using both hands, slammed his head through the wall.

Violet struggled to stand. Her arm gave her grief. She lifted herself up with her other arm to see Amraam attempt to fight Pandora. Violet watched as he sustained another blow to the head. Pandora grabbed the dagger from his shoulder and torqued it sideways. He dropped from the pain. As Pandora removed the blade she shoved him to the floor with a sickening thud. Violet could not believe it. All of them were down, again. And Pandora was unscathed. Then Violet heard footsteps. They were slow and steady coming from behind her. Violet turned her sight from Pandora and onto Oracle.

Uncertainty filled her. She closed her eyes to pray that Oracle and Pandora were not going to finish them off. She opened her eyes to see Oracle standing above her, looking down at her. "Oracle, please. Don't."

Oracle tilted her head. "A guardian angel is watching. You should remain down."

Violet was puzzled, unsure of what Oracle was trying to say. Violet doubted her and watched as she stepped towards Pandora.

The two were in a deadlocked stare. Violet remained on edge. The rest of the team was on the floor. Her mind was put at ease for a second as Pandora faced Oracle and then lunged for her. Pandora moved with lightning speed, Romeo's dagger in her hand. Violet was amazed that Oracle dodged every move, her hands remaining at her side. Pandora attempted a grab but Oracle dodged it. As Pandora swung the blade, Oracle seemed to miss it by the fine hair on her face. Violet, instead of feeling fear for Oracle as a traitor, felt the urge to fight alongside her sister in arms.

Pandora started to gain the upper hand. Oracle then avoided another slash and dodged to get behind Pandora. Violet could see thin red slits on Oracle's face and neck as she stepped back towards the end of the hall near the window. Violet tried to stand but felt her arm give out once again. Oracle appeared to be slowing down. Violet took a deep breath and lifted herself up from the floor. Her right arm dangled. She knew it was broken. She stumbled towards them, noticing that Oracle and Pandora were locked into a struggle. Pandora was slowly beginning to inch the blade closer to Oracle's chest. Violet could see Oracle was losing the fight. She began to run but then saw Oracle jerk her head to the left. At the same moment, Pandora looked up and tilted her head to the right. Violet saw the window behind them shatter and blood splatter along the wall. Romeo's dagger clanging against the floor.

Pandora stepped back and looked down at her hand. Her arm cast a shadow on the floor. Violet noticed a small hole through it and her small watch had been destroyed. She heard a small tune in her ear. Comms were back on.

"Good morning everyone."

She heard the voice of the guardian angel Oracle had talked about. "Crosshair!" She rejoiced. Oracle made a move and grabbed Pandora by the wounded hand. Pulling her in. As she pulled her, Violet charged forward and helped Oracle by pushing Pandora over into the broken window frame. Pandora's back hit the broken glass as half of her body now hung out of the window. She made an attempt to grab Violet but her fingers whisked by her hair. Violet pulled Oracle back.

"Get away from the window!" Radical announced. He threw a small charge onto the wall below the window.

Violet leaped backwards with Oracle in her hands. Pandora used her legs to pull herself back into hall quickly as she avoided a second shot by Crosshair. Then the blast shook the floor. Violet felt a wave of heat as she and Oracle collided with the floor. The blast was not huge, but precise. She looked to see the bottom of the wall knocked outwards. Pandora still standing but off balance from the blast.

Violet was petrified. Pandora was still standing. Then suddenly, she saw Romeo drive his dagger upward into Pandora's chest. He shoved the dagger deep but to his surprise, she grabbed his hand and performed a trip take down. She drove her hand into his throat and floored him. She stood there, no emotion, no sense of pain. She looked down at the dagger and pulled it out of herself. Romeo flinched as another bullet from Crosshair found its way through her chest. Pandora looked straight ahead. She appeared unfazed by anything. She lifted her hand, and threw the knife at Romeo. He managed to dodge the blade as it grazed his cheek and stuck into the floor.

Violet stared in disbelief as the woman was still not dead. Then her body jolted and began to fall back. She could see Pandora's mid-section start to dissolve in an orange glow. Pandora fell back and over the busted ledge. It must have been some kind of dissolving agent similar to the Adrenaline Solution. A radical form of combustion that triggered once a team member died. To get rid of any evidence of their existence. Violet let her breath out slowly and looked over at Oracle, "Thank you."

Oracle cracked a smile, "You withhold doubts."

Violet realized Oracle did have a gift. Her feelings towards her started to ease. But Violet still carried doubt in her mind, "Are you really the third? One of them?"

Oracle's blank stare shook from left to right, "No."

"Why'd you run off and disappear?" Violet held some hope for her.

Oracle fixed her stare at Violet, "Sometimes, silence brings me clarity and allows for clear communication with others."

The moans of wounded teammates caught Violet's attention. She figured that Oracle's riddle would be solved soon enough if she put more thought into it. But right now, the injured came first. She released Oracle and shot up to assess the rest of her team. She looked towards the end of the hallway. The damaged wall and missing window seemed quiet now. Violet approached the edge of the hall carefully. She held onto her broken arm, ready for anything. Romeo stood up with her and grabbed his blade. Both looked down to the ground, ready in case Pandora was still alive. A glimpse of her body seemed to be glowing orange. Her body was rapidly dissolving.

Romeo laid his hand on Violet's shoulder. "Finally, light at the end of the tunnel."

She smiled at him, then heard Gothica's moan. She turned to commence her job as medic. Kneeling down to assess Gothica's wound; Violet could tell she was in bad shape. "It's deep."

"I'll be fine, dear." Gothica struggled to speak.

"You need medical attention soon. I can start treatment, but you're gonna need a hospital soon. The Ark's infirmary."

"Already on its way." Motherboard walked over to them as she helped Radical up. "On the roof in five."

She acknowledged her and pulled out her medical stick to start the healing process. "This may by uncomfortable."

Gothica grinned, "Go ahead." Her body reacted from the shooting pain as the medicine was administered.

"This should be enough for a few minutes." Violet cupped Gothica's face. "Just hold on."

Violet turned to look at Romeo, who stared at his blade and then at Gothica. The blood soaked weapon finally found its owners hands. He rubbed the blade against his thigh to wipe the blood from it and slid it back into his sheath. He looked at his fallen comrade and bent down. "Come on, someone needs to bring this gothic mess to good health."

"I still need to look at your wound?" Violet examined his collar bone area, the bolt was still lodged there. She assessed his stance and could tell that putting weight on his leg was causing him a great deal of pain.

"I'll live." He picked Gothica up and hobbled down the hallway.

Violet noticed Amraam holding his arm and rubbing his face, "Are you doing okay?" She asked with a faint smile.

Amraam smiled back. "As for the chirping birds around my head, yeah. Are you?" He nodded his head at her.

Violet seemed to forget about her arm. She assessed her injury and felt around, "Probably a fracture. I can still move it, though."

Amraam looked around the hall, "How come this place isn't crawling with police, yet?"

Motherboard spoke up, "Well, someone had to buy us some time to take care of that psycho woman."

"How'd you do that?" Amraam was intrigued.

"I tampered with the call center reports. Enough to buy us some time, but it won't be long till this place is flooded with police though. That's why I called in the Ark to pick us up as soon as that woman dangled from the window."

Violet felt a sense of pride in her team. "Thanks, Motherboard."

"You're welcome." Motherboard held Radical's arm over her shoulder, "Can you not help but get your ass kicked by girls?"

Radical laughed, "Must be my explosive personality, girls seem to fall for it."

"You should let me look at you," Violet reached into her medical pouch and pulled out another medical stick. "I can stop the bleeding and give your body some relief."

"Fine," Motherboard wiped her face, "It's not that deep." She adjusted her glasses. A long streak of blood reached from her forehead to her jaw. It was more severe as it had slit across her nose. A small slit made its way across the left lens of her glasses.

Violet looked at the wound, "Here," She dragged the stick across her face, the bleeding slowed. She looked at Radical, "You?"

"I think I'll need a chiropractor. Neck is a little sore." He rubbed the back of his neck.

"We can take care of it in the Ark. But we need to get moving to the roof." Violet watched the two proceed down the hallway following Romeo. She turned around to look out the window. "Crosshair, are you there?"

"Yes ma'am. Still watching."

Violet could feel her emotions flooding in. "You saved us."

"Just doing my job. Sorry, I took so long, had to get a good shot." Crosshair's words were comforting.

Violet smiled as a tear poured down her cheek, "You have nothing to be sorry for."

Amraam walked up to her, holding his arm. "Crosshair, how'd you know where we were?"

He chuckled over comms. "Can't explain it really. A voice in head was talking to me. A strange feeling showing me you guys were in trouble and it led me here." Crosshair ended transmission.

Violet looked at Amraam, confused for a second, then she looked over at Oracle who stood over the ledge. "It was her. That's what she meant about the silence and clarity. She was helping Crosshair find us."

Amraam held Violet close to him, "Guess Reaper was right about her. Glad she's on our side."

Violet watched as the mysterious woman stared outside. The sounds of police sirens began to fill the night air. The mission was complete. She took into account her teammates. Feeling the comforting embrace of Amraam's hand, made her realize it was going to be okay. With the exception of the wounded, their work here was done. "Speaking of, where is Reaper?" She grew worried.

Oracle turned to face them. Small slits scattered around her face and neck. Her marble eyes gazed at them. "He is alive. Death conquered the ghost."

Chapter 26

The Nest was filled with laughter. After two days of recovery, bedrest, and mourning those who passed on, it was time to throw a celebration. The team had come together and had overcome a trying mission. Together, they succeeded, and together they would celebrate a victory. The Nest had music playing with the added bonus of Circuitcrusher giggling away as he entertained them. Unable to leave his quarters from being in the infirmary, he entertained as a large projection on the wall of the cafeteria. Still bumbling around with the camera, he debated his next device, "I don't know whether or not comfort or style is more important when selecting automated handicap transportation." The camera he used shot all around as if he had no idea how to handle it. After nearly a week on medication and nerve repair, Circue still slurred his speech.

Monster was in the crowd teasing him over the Nest's speaker system. "What do you know about style?" The rest laughed.

Circue giggled, still loopy from being on the pain killers. "I know better than to choose something more than anything in style. Nobody seems to be complaining about the new suits?"

Reaper laughed. Grateful that he made it through another recovery tank operation. His back was going to need more work and the road to recovery and gaining movement in his legs would still be far. Most importantly, he was alive and braver than ever. Still maintaining his role in the team, trying to improve their equipment and making them laugh, even from bedside. Violet had done a great job in treating him and getting him back to normal as quickly as possible. She was another, against all odds, that had come through for the team. Reaper was impressed by her. Never giving up and still keeping her faith in them. Something he finally was getting the hang of. Her confidence was beginning to be contagious. And Reaper knew that it was important for that to finally spread throughout the team.

Reaper began to admire each of them. Proud of them for what they do. It was by them united, they were able to accomplish what seemed impossible. And another person that restored his own confidence and what could have been his best recruitment decision to date, and not a moment too late, Oracle. She caught his attention as he surveyed the room. She seemed to be staring at him. During the last few days, she had made a stop by his room. Feelings were something that could not be hidden, after all. But she made him understand that they could be suppressed when they needed to be. There was a time and a place for them. A time when they could allow themselves to be human. He smiled at her but was quickly caught off guard as she smiled back. He knew by now that he could not hide from what she saw. Her abilities proved to be the turning point in their battle against Provost's other team. But the realization that she was gifted without the aid of any Solution, made him think. Could it have been fate?

Reaper looked out the window that overlooked the mountain outside. Just a short trail down, laid the remains of Boss. The man with good advice, intense focus, and undying support. Next to him, Provost's remains lie buried beneath the dirt. Their leader, who taught them to fight for what was right and to never stop or accept a thanks. A man that Reaper felt, entrusted the Cleansing Blade before his dying breath. Now they were gone, and it was time to take control and move forward with the reformed Cleansing Blade. But something still felt like it needed to be done. There was still a task at hand.

Reaper watched her near the punchbowl and tea dispenser. Gothica was fixing herself a drink. He observed her make a turn too fast and flinched. She was still healing from the wound in her stomach. Her being close to death, had made him realize it was time to not take opportunities for granted. And this was his second chance to let go of the guilt and thanks to Violet's strong will and medical skills, Gothica had survived. He looked to Violet, how much stronger she had become after their lives had changed again. It was different to not see her caress her braid, but the shorter hair tied back made her seem stronger. Next to her, Amraam sat with his arm around her shoulders. His deep laughter echoed throughout the lounge. Reaper had no reason to tell them that having feelings for one another was bad. He kept his mouth shut, learning from Oracle's advice. Dealing with bad guys and then dealing with emotion were two different things. When stacked against a person, emotion will win every time. Reaper glanced over at Romeo, who for the first time in a long time, was laughing. Had he finally moved on? Did he finally start the healing process in his mind?

Each seemed to have matching slings and bandages around their wounds. The healing process was dramatically sped up do to their cutting edge medicine and the Adrenaline Solution. Their physical injuries would be healed within the week. Due to another member, they were able to all have escaped with their lives. Reaper looked at the man that pulled them from the fire yet again, Crosshair. He had claimed some kind of voice told him that the team was in trouble. Oracle had disappeared from their sensors to be alone in order to lead Crosshair right to the perfect position. She had done what many would see as impossible, and showed Crosshair the way to save the others from Pandora's wrath. She was the same reason he was able to clear his head momentarily and defend against Phantom's punishing strikes.

Reaper had always admired Crosshair. His skill and dedication had saved them from disaster countless times before. It gave him the hope and confidence as Cleansing Blade's now only leader. Each member was an asset that depended on one another. If there was a time it was shown perfectly, it was in New York. Crosshair had given up his time away to find himself, in order to help his team. Reaper approached him, wanting to know more about his 'time off'. "So what was normal life like?"

Crosshair rubbed his fuzzy beard, "Honestly it was harder than I remember."

"What about your father?"

"He knew immediately who I was. Never felt a hug that tight before."

Reaper was intrigued. "What did he tell you?"

"Whether or not he was telling the truth, he told me my mother had taken me from him. When she died, he didn't know how to raise me. So he figured he'd let the system take me."

"I'm sorry to hear that." Reaper felt sorry him.

"Don't worry, he begged for forgiveness." Crosshair smiled, "And I gave it to him. There's really no need to be upset about something that long ago."

Reaper nodded, "You're right. So are you here to stay? Or do you need more time?"

"I told him I worked for a company with lots of assignments. And lots of hours." Crosshair laughed, "He even told me he was proud of me."

"As am I," Reaper grinned, "Believe me."

"So, I figure I can stay here. Besides, that so called normal life is pretty hard." The two laughed. Reaper could tell Crosshair knew his place. The original Cleansing Blade would struggle more with living in society than dying in the battlefield.

Gothica set her drink down at the end of the table, catching Reaper's attention. He thought about their conversation in the tower. She knew how to live in society since she came from it. Reaper approached her, trying not to show his guilt, "How you feeling?"

"Like drinking some tea." Gothica smiled back. "You? How's the noggin?"

"Still attached." Reaper teased back. "Not sure if had I lost it, I'd be any better, though."

"Yeah, your overthinking takes a toll on the body. As does your constantly changing of battle plans and orders in the middle of a mission."

Reaper laughed at her comment. He sat next to her as he recalled their conversation in the tower. "You remember what you told me a few days ago? Up in the tower."

Gothica's smile faded, "A lot happened that night. Which part?"

"Your last words to me before you all went off to fight."

She was thinking, "About your orders?"

"Yes," Reaper grinned, "You told me you would trust my judgment, if we lived."

She looked suspicious about his words, "Yeah, that's right. I'll start to let up on you. But just a little."

"Appreciated," Reaper fought to find the appropriate words to say next. "With that being said, I think it's time for you to leave us."

"Excuse me?" She was thrown off. "If that was supposed to come out nicely, you failed."

"Gothica, listen to me," Reaper looked into her pale blue eyes. "You have a life. Outside of all of this. You know what you want, you have a family. Your mom, maybe even your fiancé."

"I get it," She responded, "You want to protect me?"

Reaper smiled, "Yes, I do." He flashed to the sight of Aurora, years before. Wishing he had done something to save her. He did not want to relive the moments, so cleared his head and looked back at Gothica. "Aurora died in field, and I know that's part of the job. But I at least have a chance with you. I think that taking your past and your home for granted is foolish. What you had, what you still can have, is something that only some of us could ever dream of."

"I hate it when you're philosophical." She smiled, her eyes were getting watery. "Did Crosshair open your eyes or what?"

"He deserves to see what he used to be. But he knows he can't have that again. You can." he pleaded.

She rubbed her eye before a tear slipped by. "Don't need me anymore, huh?"

"You lived to see us all fight against impossible odds. We come here, train, sleep, eat, and then fight again. I don't," Reaper paused to look around, then back at her, "I don't want that for everyone. You should love someone, maybe have children. Whatever it is that's normal."

Gothica looked down, she was fighting back tears.

"I want Gothica to rest. And Alice, I want you to live on." He recalled Oracle's words to Romeo. How Julia wanted him to live on. To move on without looking back. Something that was taken for granted. He placed his hand on her arm.

"What will you do?" She whispered.

"The only thing I know how. I can't live outside these walls. For my own sake and the world's. But you can. And if you trust my judgement, it says for you to be, Alice Marshall again."

She shook her head and looked up at him. The room seemed to quiet down as everyone noticed them.

"Uh oh," Radical said to interrupt them, "What's wrong now?"

The two stood up. "I have an announcement." Everyone turned to face them.

"Marriage?" Circue mumbled.

"Crosshair has brought to my attention the importance of something. Something more than all of this. He showed me that there is a life beyond this Nest, maybe for all of us one day, but certainly for a few." He looked at them. "Amraam, Radical," He nodded at her, "Motherboard. Even Oracle. You all have had the chance to have families and lives before this. Normal lives. Let me introduce you to this young lady," He turned Alice. "This is Alice Marshall. Has a mom, and fiancé. And she deserves to live that life she had. So, for anyone here who wishes to go back, may do so." The room was silent. "What Philip Johnson took from some of us, we can't have back. But you all still can."

Motherboard spoke up, "Let me get Alice's life back on track then. I'll be in the briefing room setting her up to live in this world again."

"And IIII'lll help," Circue interrupted as he readjusted the screen. "We'll have you back to normal in no time." With that Motherboard nodded and left the room.

Reaper took that as a sign that Motherboard had made her decision to stay. He looked over at Radical who threw up his hand, "I made too many mistakes in that life. I can't really go back to that right now. This unit seems to need someone willing to be a little crazy anyway. Besides," he turned to watch Motherboard leave the room, "This is my second chance."

"Amraam?" Reaper looked over at Violet who held Amraam closer to her.

Amraam looked back at her, "Honestly, what I had back home was worth fighting for." He looked back at Reaper, "And here, I'm better equipped to fight for it."

Reaper watched as Violet smiled and held his arm. He looked at everyone and back at Alice. "Then let's live on. And give Alice here everything she needs to return."

"I don't know what to say now," Alice spoke softly, "Why?"

Reaper turned to her, "Feelings, they make you care. Sometimes," he looked over at Oracle, "They can be difficult to hide." He held Alice's shoulder, "And I detect that deep down, you want to go back."

Alice wiped her face, "I would be lying if I said no." She hugged him and looked over to Violet. "Shall we then?" She padded Reaper on the shoulder and followed Violet and Amraam out. Violet held her hand as they left the room.

"Deep." Romeo interrupted the silence. "Why don't we get a pass to leave?"

Reaper looked over at him and Monster. "Because you know as well as I do that we can't."

Chapter 27: Epilogue

The hall was quiet. Reaper watched as Alice was dressed in normal clothing and a back pack on her shoulder. She was tightly embracing Violet who shared tears of goodbye. She looked over at Amraam. He too had been recruited at the same time. Together, they had both lived through the Rival Sinai incident and were reborn from it.

"Well, it was fun." Amraam smiled at her. "Good luck out there. It was a privilege to fight at your side."

Alice smiled, "As it was to fight on yours." She turned to look at Romeo, who stood with a grin on his face.

He crossed his arms, "Not sure what I'll do when I can't wake up and see your pale mug around the Nest anymore." He teased.

"Guess you'll just have to look in the mirror more often." She laughed. Romeo stuck his hand out to shake hers.

"Nice to have you on our side." He told her as they shook hands.

Motherboard walked down the hallway to meet up with the crowd near the Ark's bay doors. "We've got Alice Marshall's life back on track. Even dealt with the death certificate. You'll be able to start your new life. And, I got you a nice position at the NSA branch in record holdings."

"Thanks," Alice smiled, her eyes watering as she looked at the last person to say goodbye to.

Reaper looked at her, "Thanks for everything, Alice. I couldn't have done much without your help." He stuck his hand out but she moved to embrace him.

"It was my pleasure." She held him tight. "Thank you, Reaper." The two released. "If you ever need me, you'll know where to look. Back home." She smiled, wiping her face, "Wow, that sounds good. And a little strange."

Reaper smiled at her. "Enjoy it. And don't look back."

"Good luck to you all," Alice said as she turned to walk into the Ark. It would take her to her own home. Just as it would take the Cleansing Blade from their home to their mission, and back. He watched as Alice walked inside and never turned around. The bay door shut.

The halls of the Nest were quiet. After a full day of partying, and the departure of Reaper's mentor, it was a bittersweet evening. He stared at the picture on his ceiling. Aurora would have been proud of him. He had finally found closure.

"Restless minds, never find sleep."

Reaper grinned at the sound of Oracle's voice, "It's hard to sleep sometimes."

She moved her head from his chest and looked up at him. "We are home, now." Oracle spoke softly. "No longer in the hollow. You should find sleep easier."

"I wish that were the case." Reaper moved his hand up Oracle's arm to hold her close. "I didn't thank you yet. You really did save us out there."

"As long as I am here," Oracle whispered, "Your gratitude makes no difference."

Their lips met in a gentle kiss. Reaper was finally allowing himself to feel. He set his head back into his pillow as the two lay there still. Was this what happiness felt like? He immediately thought of Alice. Though she lived, she was gone per his request.

"You allow restlessness." Oracle broke through his thoughts, reading him even still.

He could not resist, "I hope I made the right decision."

"Leadership is never easy," She whispered softly, "But giving a second chance to those who deserve it, should be."

He knew she supported his decision. Alice had contemplated home for a while. After their last mission, it was time for her to follow what she truly wanted. He thought of her, "Oracle, will she be happy?"

"You ask questions, to the answers you already know."

Reaper smiled, "Good then."

Romeo sipped slowly on his cup of morning tar. His coffee was stronger this morning. The Nest was waking up, members wandering from the showers to the training room. He enjoyed the silence of the briefing room before it was invaded by the others. He looked over to where Boss would stand. The smell of cigarette was missing. He found himself thinking of him. His sayings to help them adapt. He thought about the Academy. That dark place returned to his memory, Provost appearing out of the darkness. Romeo looked at him, but he did not feel angry. Instead, he felt pity. The man had trained them, resurrected them into the new life they were forced to live. Only to lay dead on the floor by his other creation. The dagger on the floor covered in Provost's blood. All he could do was watch as Provost tried to speak to him. The fear in his eyes, the remorse in his face. Maybe he did regret betraying them.

He, along with the team had shared that blade's edge. Oracle had been right. It did contain the blood of his team mates and of his former leader, but it also shared the blood of that woman, Pandora. He took a breath and let it slowly before taking another sip. He set his cup down and looked over at his weapon rack, his dagger hung from its sheath. The blade was clean now. After the mission, Romeo took the time to wash it from its stains. While he did, he carved another word onto the blade, "on".

He looked around the weapon rack and noticed another's. Her crossbow hung from its place. He thought about her, about what she would do after her experiences here. As much as he hated to admit it, he found himself missing her. She had taught them a lot. And for the first time in a while, he accepted Reaper's decision to allow her to leave. Maybe she deserved that. Just as he found himself nearly appreciative of Oracle and Reaper's decision about her. Maybe, the Cleansing Blade was getting stronger.

He was shaken out of his trance as the briefing room doors opened. Violet walked over to the coffee machine. "Good morning." She greeted him with her bright smile. "Sleep well?"

"Like a log," Romeo grumbled, "I take it you did."

"Yes," Violet pressed the button to the machine, "Yesterday was fun."

"Don't hear that word too much around here." Romeo sipped from his dark drink.

"What? Fun?" Violet adjusted the mixture of her drink. "We should have more of it around here. It's rejuvenating. Helps keep us inspired, too. You know, we gotta stay inspired."

"Yeah," Romeo remembered those words before. His mind thought of Julia. He knew her and Violet would have made great friends. Both cared about others, something he was not accustomed to in a very long time. Boss would tell them to enjoy the little things. And if anyone was filling his shoes, it was Violet.

She turned to face him with her sweet beverage in hand. Romeo allowed a small grin and raised his cup. She nodded and raised hers back. She then proceeded to take a drink. He looked down at his cup. An image of Julia's old photo seemed to reflect atop the dark coffee. He took a deep breath and let it out as the image dissolved within the black liquid.

"Well, see you in the training circuit." Violet nodded and proceeded towards the doors. Her hands ran through her hair. Romeo observed her. Her short hair was bizarre to him. She no longer had her braid. Maybe because she no longer needed it.

About the Author

Randolph grew up in New Mexico and still lives there with his wife and child. This novel marks his third publication. A novel that he states is very personal to him.

Author's works:

Cleansing Blade Saga: Internal Fear Project

Cleansing Blade Saga 2: Camelot's Dream

Cleansing Blade Saga 3: Merciless Destinies

Made in the USA
Middletown, DE
26 October 2018